Crestfallen Queen

D. M. Walker

Crestfallen Queen

Vanguard Press

VANGUARD PAPERBACK

© Copyright 2024
D. M. Walker

The right of D. M. Walker to be identified as author of
this work has been asserted by her in accordance with the
Copyright, Designs and Patents Act 1988.

All Rights Reserved

No reproduction, copy or transmission of this publication
may be made without written permission.
No paragraph of this publication may be reproduced,
copied or transmitted save with the written permission of the
publisher, or in accordance with the provisions
of the Copyright Act 1956 (as amended).

Any person who commits any unauthorised act in relation to
this publication may be liable to criminal
prosecution and civil claims for damages.

A CIP catalogue record for this title is
available from the British Library.

ISBN 978 1 83794 158 2

This is a work of fiction. Names, characters, businesses, places, events
and incidents are either the product of the author's imagination or used in a
fictitious manner. Any resemblance to actual persons, living or dead, or actual
events is purely coincidental.

Vanguard Press is an imprint of
Pegasus Elliot Mackenzie Publishers Ltd.
www.pegasuspublishers.com

First Published in 2024

Vanguard Press
Sheraton House Castle Park
Cambridge England

Printed & Bound in Great Britain

I dedicate this book to Michael for always inspiring me to keep going and staying with me along the way.

Chapter 1

Lina walks down the dirt road on her tiptoes, watching her shadow to check her movements. It's just passed midday … she wipes a bead of sweat from her forehead and adjusted her basket to her hip. Her dress slightly tattered at the ends and the dirty apron began to dampen from the moisture of the freshly laundered linen she carried along. It's not a long walk to the river from her home on the outskirts of town but Lina takes her time. She is in no hurry to be home where she will be doing chores until nightfall at least. Lina looks around the deserted road and stops for a moment to listen. She turns to set down her basket on the tall grass beside the road, then stands upright, closes her eyes and strains her ears. She takes a deep breath in and smells the damp soil from last month's rains still settling in the dirt. She hears the wind whipping the tops of the tallest oak trees. She strains harder and far off hears the unmistakable sounds of town like the light chatter of people bustling around. She hears the quiet of the woods surrounding her, and the impetuous noises of its inhabitants.

Lina looks down at her plain brown itchy dress and slightly torn up poorly-sustained shoes. She slouches down to scratch off a bit of dirt stuck to her stained apron only to see the ground rematerialize beneath her. Blinking profusely she slowly rights herself and raises her head up straight. She drew in a deep breath as she realized that she was no longer in the woods. She was no longer a tattered peasant doing chores. Lina looked up at the beautiful marble hall and down at the rich thick royal carpet she stood on. It was the biggest room she had ever been in, and it was filled with flowers and silver and beautiful, sparkly things. She looked down and saw herself covered in a beautiful soft-pink silky dress that clung perfectly to her shape. Her matching slightly heeled shoes lifted her up angelically causing her to want to spin on the spot so that her dress cascaded out around her. Applause rang out from all the finely dressed people whom she hadn't noticed gathering around her.

All the people dressed well enough for a royal wedding clapping for me, she mused.

"Princess?"

A very tall and handsome man with dark hair bends to a low bow while extending his hand to Lina who smiles and reaches for his hand.

*Clip-clop, clip-clop, clip-clop, clip-clop.

In an instant just as it had come, everything had fallen away. The room was gone, the applause a distant memory and the prince remained a dream. Lina scrambled to pick up her basket and hide in the cover of the trees. She runs far enough to see the road still but to easily be hidden. she squats down by a log and waits for the horse and its owner to appear. She sees them arrive and pass. She does not move until the hooves fade away in the distance for fear of weary travelers and their various needs. Once certain the person has moved on, she scoops up her basket and makes her way back slowly to the road listening intently for others unwanted. Everyone knows the forest can be more dangerous than the roads. The roads have men, but the forest has men and beasts.

Lina spares a small thought to her father and the last night of his life. The sounds of the growling and the desperation in his screams. But the screams were nothing compared to the silence that followed. It was the sharpest silence she had ever experienced. The silence so loud it hurt her ears and split her head with pain. Lina pushed the thoughts from her mind and with both a heavy sigh and a heavy heart she continued home to do her chores.

Lina makes it to the edge of Crestfallen village and looks at her home. It was shabby, small, and just as dingy as her on first appearance. Set back from the road a bit, the home was made mostly of timber and mud with a single stone chimney stack rising from the back. When their father was about as a hunter and trapper there used to be furs of all kinds drying out on the outside of the hut. Her father, being the best hunter in quite some area, always had a large bounty to clean and sell. At the moment there were two hides up on the wall. Contributed no doubt by her brother who did what he could to take some of the hardship off her mom. Jacob couldn't hunt as well as his father but he got better all the time. Before their father died, he had taught Jacob a lot as the oldest sibling and male, Lina often wondered if he had known he would take care of them some day or if maybe he had meant for him to care for a family of his own. Just as Lina reached out and touched the soft fur of the deer hide, she heard him coming up from behind the smoke shack. In his hands two more small skins to be hung and sold, that of two black rabbits.

"Finished curing the meat then? Won't mother be happy?" Lina mused.

Jacob cracked a brilliant smile and stuck his nose up at his sister. Standing a foot-and-a-half taller than her with broad shoulders and dark hair framing his tan face and big deep brown eyes they looked like anything but siblings. Lina having a small build and long fair blonde hair with hazel eyes she has always looked different compared to her brother.

"Well if it isn't Little Lina coming to crack jokes at my expense. How was the laundry; you didn't meet anyone on the road did you?"

"I got back quick enough to finish my chores. And didn't speak to or see anyone on the road. Tell me, is she still doing good today?" The hopeful look in her eyes were snuffed out quickly with her brother's grimace.

"She brought more laundry home from Crestfallen Manor, but once home she complained about her back hurting... She took her medicine and has been in bed since," Jacob spat out the ending with clear dismay. It's nothing new for them to have to hold up their mother and spoon feed her dinner after one of her flare-ups causes her to immobilize herself. The problem was the town doctor knows this medicine doesn't help but sells it to her anyway. Now if they can't afford it she gets in a bad way and lashes out at them. It wouldn't be so terrible if he wasn't greedy and mean. He charged what he wanted... He would charge more and more all the time. Lina heard Jacob arguing with her mom once—apparently, he would drop the price if Lina would pick it up, Jacob absolutely refused. She had never heard him that angry before and hoped never to have to again. After she was told to steer completely clear of the man and warned to steer clear of any men to be safe for now. Jacob made her promise, And he looked so sad that she did. She would do anything to make sure he was never that sad again. After all, most days Jacob was the only person who really cared for her.

"When I become queen I will stop the sales of all such drugs to the people and jail any who are caught with it in market." Lina stated matter-of-fact to her brother in hopes of turning his mood to lighter thoughts.

"A noble venture for a fair queen," Jacob said then laughed and smiled at his little sister as he hung the remaining hides up to dry after cleaning them of remaining fat and filth. Once finished, Jacob looked at his sister with a seriousness that made her skin crawl a bit. She felt she had succeeded in fixing his mood and wondered what was dwelling in his mind.

"Lina... You are fifteen now and I'm starting to worry that you haven't let go of the childish fantasies and games we played when you were a younger. You keep up with your chores well enough but I still see you daydreaming when you think no one is looking sometimes—"

"Do you remember when we were camping at the waterfall all that time ago?" Lina quickly interjected.

Jacob eyed her wearily, knowing she was drawing attention away from his point on purpose, he decided to see where she was going with this...

"Yes. Approximately ten harvests or so when Father had such a big haul we were able to travel to the falls and make sales to the heads of Aliyen. We as a family have ne'er had a prouder moment in service to our kingdom."

"Do you remember the night of the harvest fire? There were people dressed up and a huge fire going and all kinds of foods? That's where we got the cake. Father bought it for us all in celebration of the year. I had never had something so..." Lina searched for the words to describe the sweet crumbling bread she was so unaccustomed to but couldn't remember well enough. Had it been rich? was it moist? She honestly couldn't be sure after so long. She shook her head to clear her thoughts.

"Anyway that was when we started playing the game. Father gave us both pieces of cake and a little cider to wash it down. When he handed mine to me, he called me Princess Lina, and he called you Sir Jacob."

"Yes, I remember Lina," Jacob interrupted with patience wearing. "We kept playing that game all the way through the trip. We played it on the way home, we played it until the night the fire went out on Father. I had to stop playing, and it's time for you to stop playing too." Now the look on Jacob's face was one of concern. He positioned his back on the wall of their hut, covered his eyes to look at the sun's position as it sunk down in the sky nearing the treetops.

"I'm serious Lina. You are nearing marrying age, honestly if Father was still alive you might have been married by now. You have to start looking at things more realistically. I want you to have a happy, good life with a decent man but I don't think Mother is going to be working much longer with her condition. Sending her walking a half hour each way to get that laundry is too much. Even with your help of washing it, We need to start talking about your future."

Lina looked past her brother, she refused to meet his eyes while she felt that hurt. While the sneaking feeling snuck up on her that he also did not believe she was a princess. Suddenly the voices of all the kids in the village rose up in her ears,

"Lollyland Lina Lollyland Lina..."

"You gunna go play in your fake castle Lina?"

"Like anyone royal would ever want you."

"Who would make a girl who looks like a dog a princess..." The laughing, the cruelty of unchecked children released on the lucky enough to dream in a place as ill-begotten as this. She never understood why wanting more was so condemnable, she never understood why she wasn't allowed to dream. She doesn't understand now why her brother suddenly lost faith in her, and quietly questioned if he ever believed or if he was just again protecting her.

"I don't know what you want me to say." Lina's eyes swam with tears as she looked away from her brother dragging her eyes to the ground.

"You always told me I could be anything I wanted," she choked out, hiding a sob.

"I meant within reason," Jacob explained and moved in to hug his little sister. He held her in a strong hug for a moment while she attempted to pull herself together, then pulled her out to arm's length away.

"We have time," he said, wiping the tears from her eyes. "Let us make dinner and prepare for the next day. You know the kitchen makes a fool of me."

Jacob reached into his pocket and pulled out a piece of jerky and held it to his sister as a peace offering. She took it sniffling slightly and wiping away the last few tears. She knew he would need his help in the kitchen for sure, so she went towards the back of their humble home and entered with Jacob. Once inside she put the stew pot over the fire and asked Jacob to go get water from the well. she cut up the rabbit meat he had left for dinner along with potatoes, mushrooms, carrots, some wild onions and a variety of herbs and spices she had scavenged through the morning and had drying inside. She placed in a bit of fat and the meat and let that cook down a bit then added the water and the vegetables. Jacob watched in awe as she fanned the fire to bring it all to a rolling boil. The smell of delicious rabbit stew began wafting through their little hut.

It was a rich meal for such a poor family, and they knew they were lucky considering.

With dinner cooking, Lina decided to go check on her mother, she instructed Jacob to keep an eye on the fire for a moment and she walked down the single hallway to one of the only three rooms the house contained. Lina entered the room and saw their mother lying motionless on one of the two beds in the small home. She leaned in to listen and make sure she was breathing. She saw the chest heave slightly up and down with labored deep breaths. She looked at her eyes and saw them flicking back and forth beneath their lids, she was dreaming. Lina felt guilty sometimes because she understood that living in a dream can be so much better than reality, but she would never dream like this. She would never allow this to be her, checked out and unavailable. She checked her blankets and found she messed herself beneath the multiple raggedy covers.

Lina diligently went and grabbed the wash basin and mop bucket and began stripping the blankets to clean them and her mother up. Her mother didn't stir until she got her off the bed to wash her properly off the mess. When she woke, she thrashed about crying fighting off some villain who didn't actually seem to be there. Lina patiently calmed her and put a cleanish damp rag to her forehead, humming a song she used to sing to her as a child. It took a while but eventually her mother lolled back into a semi drug-induced coma in her arms. Lina took care to finish cleaning her and the bed before asking Jacob to help get her back in the bed. She had to switch with the only clean blankets they had left but got her comfortable enough for the time being.

Upon going back into the kitchen Lina turned to the fire and the stew to make sure it was cooking through. Just at the moment that she bent over the heath she heard a knock, she turned to the door and grinned.

"Fancy meeting you here, say, you wouldn't have an extra spot of stew that me and my brother could nibble on, would you? I brought your brother a treasure as trade, something that I happened to come by..."

Adaleen and Jasper stood in the doorway. Adaleen was barely taller than Lina, with long, dark hair that she kept tied in a bun or a braid usually and dark clothes she said to keep her in the shadows. Jasper was the same height with the same color hair as they were identical twins except for the eyes—Jasper's were wide and compassionate, Adaleen's were sharp and distrusting. Adaleen held out a very fine-looking knife, much too nice for her to have just 'come by'. Lina smiled and ushered them in as Jacob entered the now almost full room. Adaleen and Jasper sat at the small table and laid the knife out for Jacob, who carefully picked it up and turned it over in his hands.

"And who have you stolen this from?" he asked eyeing Jasper and Adaleen carefully. Being the only actual orphans in the area, these siblings had a habit of trouble and a drive to take risks.

"No one who will come looking for it anyway," Jasper said with a laugh.

"We won it fair and square, didn't we sis?"

"Sure did, bloke really thought he could out strength my shootin', little did he know I learned from your pa so I learned from the best around!"

Lina and Jacob smiled as they spoke of their father in high regard. Adaleen and Jasper had been regulars for dinner time with them before Lina could remember. Lina and Jacob's father had been friends with Jasper and Adaleen's father and when their parents never came back from a market run, he taught them just as he had taught Jacob. He made sure they could survive and always had a warm meal a day.

Jacob set the knife in front of Jasper. They need not pay to join dinner at this house. It was merely a sign of respect to ask for entry and offer a trade, even though their places had already been set.

"It's not quite my style, but thank you. Actually, Jasper would you like to help me check the traps in the valley tomorrow? I haven't made it out there in a couple of days."

"Sure Jacob, anything to help ya out."

"Would you like some help with your gathering or are you all stocked up for now?" Adaleen asked Lina as she carried over the stew pot to the table.

"Actually I think I have plenty of what we need for now," Lina said thinking about her stores fleetingly.

"Good, I was actually hoping you would accompany me to the market to sell this knife, if we get some decent money for it, we could put it to good use," she said matter-of-fact. Lina looked to her brother to make sure he wouldn't be upset with her if she chose to go, he didn't meet her eyes but nodded slightly. Jacob knew she was just as safe with Jasper and Adaleen as she was with him. They looked at her as a little sister and him as an older brother. Whether this was because people treated them bad for being orphans or twins, he didn't know.

"Also, I tucked away a wee surprise in case you were planning stew..." Jasper had the slickest smirk on his face as he reached in his shabby bag and pulled out a loaf of fresh bread.

"Now that we did steal, but no one saw us, Jacob.""

Jacob started to scold Adaleen. "We aren't fresh to the market after all..." she added with a laugh that shook the whole room and filled it with giggles and happiness.

Lina began to scoop scalding hot bowls of rabbit stew into the bowls as the twins split the bread into five decent sized pieces, respectfully not forgetting their mother and optimistic she will want or need the food. Jacob set the bowl and food for their mother to the side and poured water into their shabby little cups to wash down their dinner. With the table set, they finally sat and began eating.

"What time are you planning on heading to the market, Adaleen?"

"Early I suppose, want to be in before the rush of the day." Adaleen blew on her stew and attempted to use the roughly carved wooden spoon set next to her. After one unsatisfyingly small bite, she abandoned the spoon and picked up the bread to dip it in. Jasper and Jacob were drinking the stew right out of the bowl and groaning from the heat.

"Relax, there is more, eat slower!" Lina told her brother, concern etching her delicate features.

"Right, right, sorry Lina, Just a long day and your cooking is hard to eat slow!" Jacob stopped his abrupt gulping at the stew and also picked up the bread. Jasper merely lowered his bowl enough to drink and burn himself a bit more slowly.

"Well this is quite the meal, fit for the queen herself," Adaleen said giving Lina a wink. Adaleen knew all about Lina's dreams. She played along with her all growing up, calling her Milady and making her crown of wildflowers. Lina smiled to herself grateful to have one person who has always indulged her fantasy. Adaleen fully believed life is what you make it, which is why she dreamed of an adventure. Lina blew on her soup and pulled pieces of her bread to eat as she looked around her table. With all the smiles and happiness, she couldn't help but think she was very rich in some ways already.

After dinner the twins bid goodnight with a promise to arrive early in the morrow and departed into the night to their respected hideout. Lina, who had already hung the laundry from the previous wash earlier still had to take the blankets out of her other room. Then she went and set her food on the bedside table and attempted to rouse her to consciousness. Her mother woke and was calm as her daughter gave her bread and water and bits of stew. She was holding it all down, which was good news for the night. She ate a decent amount and refused any more, so Lina propped her up on herself and had her move around a little. Her mother pushed her away and grabbed at the bed for support.

"I'm fine, I'm fine Lina... won't you let me go to the bathroom..." Lina shrank to the wall as her mother attempted to regain her balance. She put her right foot forward and tried to put weight on it, her leg crumbled under her, and she fell to the floor with a cry of pain. Lina lunged forward to help as Jacob opened the door and asked if she needed help.

"Gerald, Gerald please I need to use the bathroom." She reached out to Jacob. Jacob, sensing a tantrum coming, stepped in and lifted his mother with ease off the ground carrying her from the room. Lina fixed the bed up again and retrieved the bowl and cup. As Jacob carried their mother back to bed, he told Lina to wait in the kitchen for a moment.

Lina waited for her brother to come back. She looked around the dark, dirty, little kitchen and took note of everything quickly. The herbs hanging from the ceiling, the vegetables in the cabinet, the table made of shabby wood. There was a single standing cabinet on the wall across from the fireplace hearth, next to the hallway. It was so out of place, made out of fine oak and carved carefully with a beautiful ornate design. It belonged in a manor, or palace somewhere and she wasn't sure how it had ended up here. She blinked and when she opened her eyes, the room around her began to melt away. The dark room became brighter as the room's wall slid into place and the ceiling raised itself into high banister ceilings. The wood was bright, the fireplace huge, and her shabby cabin had turned into a beautiful royal hunter's cabin. She suddenly noticed she felt heavy and reached up to feel the soft fur shawl of beautiful fox. Her pale-yellow hair shinned next to the bright red and black fur. Beneath the shawl a beautiful red dress that was light and flowy came down showing a peak of black tights making it a perfect ensemble. She looked at her bare feet and saw she was standing on a giant bear rug and not far away was her handsome prince, extending his hand with a curious look on his face. Lina,

    refusing to blink in case he should disappear extended her hand and leaned forward to fall into the arms of her prince…

"What are you doing" asked Jacob as he walked in on his sister randomly diving at the ground.

"Uh nothing, just waiting like you asked…" Lina answered as she turned as red as the fox's fur had been.

"Right, look, what we talked about earlier, I came off a lot harsher than I meant to. Lina, I just need you to understand, you're a woman now. And I'm not saying I won't go as far as I have to find you the right suitor, but it will make me feel a lot better knowing you're going to be taken care of no matter what. Now that's not to say you won't have some say in the matter, but it has come time for you to start considering options. I might have you travel with me when I go to different markets, maybe the person isn't here but can be found. Either way I need you to be an adult about this." Jacob finished saying what he had to and couldn't meet Lina's eyes. Was he afraid she would cry again?

She could tell that every word he said hurt him. It killed him to tell her to grow up, it killed him to tell her to give up her dream. But she knew he was right, At this point she was just a girl who does laundry and can cook along with other basic house work, hardly qualifies to be a queen.

"I understand…" She had to try like hell to hold back her tears at the idea of letting everything she wanted go. "I'll do my best."

"Thank you, Lina, you probably shouldn't stay up late… early rise for us both." Jacob hugged his sister and left for the only other unoccupied room in the hut. Lina slept with her mother, if she got too bad, she slept on the floor. Lina looked around her at the shabby room again. Her eyes stopped on the cabinet again, she couldn't help but feel like she was like that cabinet, like the one thing in the room that didn't belong. She shook her head and walked off eagerly to go to bed, for at least at night she was still allowed to dream.

Chapter 2

The next morning Lina woke with a start before the sun was up. She had the most vivid dream the night before. It had places she had never seen before and creatures only a true prince could slay. She sat in bed trying to remember the details but as she attempted to hold onto them, they drifted from her mind. All she could say for sure is that Adaleen and Jasper had been there. She twisted in bed and saw her mother was there still sleeping with a cold sweat on her brow. Olive was in for a rough morning, as were all mornings after the medications. Lina lay in bed and closed her eyes to listen to the sounds of morning.

Somewhere not far off, a carriage was making its way down the dirt road. Chickens could be heard coming from the back of the house and Lina made a mental note to gather the eggs. They didn't have a goat or cow which would have been helpful to sell milk and make extra money, but chickens were easy to look after and cheap to feed. Listening to the birds beginning to proclaim they had found breakfast; Lina rubbed her eyes and slowly rose out of the bed. Tucking the blankets around her deep sleeping mother she brushed at her rough dirty dress. She owned very little clothing wise but decided to adorn something a little softer later on today.

Lina stretched and rubbed her back as she left the bedroom and grabbed her apron in the kitchen. The chicken coop was just next to the smoke shack. She put on her apron and made for the back door, as soon as she opened the door the bite of the crisp spring air hit her. It was chilly but it wasn't too bad and a thick dewy fog hung about in the woods behind her home. Lina wondered what all wandered in the cover of that mist, but knew it was too far off for her to worry and too weak for anything big. She trudged through the soft dirt towards the coop that her brother had reinforced against predators. She opened the makeshift gate and grabbed the chicken feed on her way in. Once inside she closed the gate and headed towards the actual little coop. The chickens began to rouse almost immediately, clucking and jumping from their respected nests. They started toward the entrance where Lina had been spreading the feed, clucking next to her feet and running past. There were only about six now, there were nine before a crafty fox came along begging for traps and reinforcement. He got a couple of chickens but in the end, they made a decent amount off his hide.

Lina began collecting the eggs absent-minded of her surroundings as she began to remember her daydream the night before. She then remembered talking to her brother. He really believed he could find her a comfortable life and loving husband even if it meant not being royal. She had to trust he had her best interest at heart, as always. Lina walked to the last of the six nests and collected two more eggs making it a total of five. she counted the eggs in her pouch and swept past the entrance to the building and the chickens now out with the sunrise. She stopped by the smoke shack and looked to see if there were any sausages. Lina found a string of venison sausage and pulled it down as Jacob entered.

"Morning..." he attempted to say through a yawn. "Ma still asleep?"

"Yes, looks as though she will be for a while," Lina answered brightly.

"I'm about to make us some breakfast: eggs and sausages to hold us off till midday."

Jacob nodded. He reached a tin cup into a bag and pulled out some coffee beans.

"Twins should be along soon, I'm gunna make some coffee." Jacob wearily and still half asleep walked out of the flap of the smoke house.

Lina stood for a moment looking at the meat they still had to sell and the skins that had been cleaned, dried and treated. She wondered if she could take a few with her to town and sell them. Jacob usually didn't trust this as he thought the marketers would try to swindle her for being so young. Then she remembered Adaleen would be there and no one in town regards her as young or naïve. Folding the sausages up carefully in her arms and walking gracefully and slow so as not to disturb the eggs, Lina followed her brother back out of the smoke house and into the house.

Once inside, she saw her brother had left for water from the well down the way. She stoked the embers of the fire and fed it some kindling to get it going. Once it was starting up, she spread it out and added more kindling to get it blazing along with two decent sized logs. On top of those she set a small metal grate and a pan with the sausages in it. She then grabbed a bowl, went to the table and started to meddle the coffee beans down before placing them in the tin pot to await their water and heat. Just then there was a knock on the door.

"You know Lina, it's supposed to be a bird that wakes early and bees that flutter about with such business at this hour," Jasper teased as he stifled a yawn.

"Let her be, if it wasn't for her motivation we wouldn't ever have breakfast or coffee." Adaleen shot at her brother elbowing him hard out of the way to enter.

"Anything I can do to help?" Adaleen asked looking hopefully at the hearth and the food sizzling.

"I got it you two just relax and try to wake up." Lina began checking the fire and stoking it again.

Jacob then entered with three buckets of water and set them down next to the table.

"Good morning, Jasper, Adaleen"

"Hey, why is it always Jasper first with you, I am a lady, am I not?" Adaleen asked with a grin on her face and sleep in her shifty eyes.

"Fiercest lady I have ever hunted with. You will try to stay out of trouble today won't you, and keep an eye on Lina?" He was pouring water in the coffee pot and setting it on the edge of the fire. They would all be more awake soon, save for Lina she couldn't stand the bitter taste.

"I'll watch her as if she were the queen herself." Adaleen put her hand up in promise that she would behave. Lina, who was busying herself with the dishes from the night before, grabbed a towel to pull the pan with sausages out and let them cool as they had been sizzling quite a while. She then carefully cracked the eggs into the same pan and scrambled them, she added a touch of salt and put the pan back over the fire to cook. Just as the coffee began to boil, she removed the coffee pot and set it on the table using the towel to protect her hand. She then placed down four small wooden mugs.

"Mornings with you two are a lot easier, I'm not sure how you make the coffee so good or what Adaleen does to ours at home that makes it so unbearable," Jasper said, taking a cup from Adaleen.

"If it's so bad, don't drink it then," Adaleen proclaimed clearly offended. Lina giggled and went to stir the eggs for an even cook, After she went and grabbed a huge plate to set them all on. They didn't have a plate for everyone so they would have to share. She set the sausages and some knives and forks on the table followed by the large plate of scrambled eggs. As usual, Jacob and Jasper dived in first. Each spearing a sausage on a fork and just grabbing a handful of scrambled eggs. Lina poured herself a cup of water and seated herself across from Adaleen. She cut about a quarter piece of a sausage and speared it herself to nibble on. Adaleen picked at the eggs with her fork occasionally bringing a bite up to her mouth. The girls always made sure the boys ate enough, as they were expected to do the heavy lifting more often than not.

After Jacob had eaten his sausage and eggs out of his hand, he relaxed back and slightly gulped at his coffee. He leaned back in his chair and finally looked ready and awake for the day.

"Thank you, Lina, that was an amazing breakfast," Jacob proclaimed with a warm smile to his sister which she returned while still nibbling at her sausage.

"Yes, very good as always, Lina," Jasper said with a toothy smile that had bits of food protruding from his cheeks. Lina laughed as Adaleen reached across and slapped her brother's leg mumbling about manners. After a bit of eating and drinking their coffee, the group rose to their feet and began stretching and talking about their plans for the day while Lina put together a plate for her mother. There would be no use trying to feed her until she wanted to wake up, so Lina left it on the table in hopes that she wouldn't sleep too long.

"Jacob, I was wondering since me and Adaleen are going to the market would you like us to sell or barter a couple of your finished hides in the shack?" Jacob leaned back and stroked his stubble on his chin looking intently at Lina.

"Huh, it would save me a trip tomorrow, and I can tell Adaleen the proper prices to fetch. I wouldn't ask you to trade as we don't need much and it's easier to lose on an unnecessary barter…" He looked off into space a moment and considered the request before nodding.

"Yea I don't see why not, As long as you allow Adaleen to do the talking. People know she sells often enough to not try to swindle her. I'll let you take a couple in if you would like."

"Great, if I'm going to be going on the road to markets with you I think it would be nice to be able to be helpful instead of just being there," Lina told her brother with conviction trying her hardest to prove she can and will be an adult from now on. She wasn't sure if she really believed she could be helpful but at the very least she could avoid being a burden.

"Well, why don't we go look and see what we can carry by ourselves, we won't take much as they get heavy. You run along and get ready Lina I'll grab the merch from Jacob." Adaleen stretched again then walked towards the backdoor, followed by Jacob and Jasper. Lina went into the hallway and back into the room she shared with her mother who was still asleep. There she went to the little corner shelf that held all four of her shabby dresses. She picked up the soft blue dress that was just slightly too big on her and felt the material. It wasn't silk but it was more than nice enough for the market they were going to. She went and grabbed the wash basin and trekked back to the kitchen to clear it and add new water, and a rag to clean up with. Lina removed her usual dirty dress and apron and folded them in the corner before washing her face and rinsing her hair in the basin. She then used the semi-clean rag to wash the dirt from her body. She cleaned her body center and was beginning to wipe away at her arms when it happened. Everything around her blanked out and then normal again. Really quickly it blacked out again as if she was closing her eyes. Then again black as she held the rag to her arm, she saw a beautiful tub of warm water arising around her. With warm mist rising up and marble walls materializing past the tub's ends.

Lina closed her eyes and shook her head. She didn't have time for dreams, she had to grow up. She shook herself until she was back, seated on her bed with a basin of water at her feet. She looked around at her life, at the nothing she had. She took in the dirty floors and poor walls and she cried a little. She shook her head again to make herself stop, crying was for little girls, and she had to be better than that now. She finished cleaning herself and slid on the light blue dress that used to belong to her mother. She was sure she looked just like her. She left the room with one last look at the woman who birthed and raised her. She was a shell of who she had been, of the woman her memory still held a candle to. She decided then and there that no matter what her brother says, she will not settle for less than love and comfort.

Lina walked back into the kitchen to find Adaleen waiting for her. She had a couple of smaller pelts they could easily carry to the market with them and a snack of venison jerky and bread to split for midday hunger pains.

"Well don't you look nice." Adaleen noted the dress and smiled at Lina.

"Thanks, I have to wash my work dress… Adaleen do you not wear dresses?" Lina looked at Adaleen's clothing and realized she had never seen her in anything other than dark colored pants.

"Na, looking fancy doesn't help with a clean get away always. Better to be dressed to run if I have to, besides where do you even hide a knife on you in that thing?" Lina looked down already knowing without an exterior sheath there was no place she could have a weapon concealed on her person.

"Well, lucky I have you with me then!" Lina replied, noting the multitude of pockets on Adaleen's pants and jacket. She began to fill a water gourd for the trip into town as Adaleen rolled up and bundled the furs. They only had to venture a few thousand feet into town to get to the market and would take the road the whole way in. Adaleen had a bag she threw over one shoulder that caught her dark gray colored jacket and pulled it back just slightly revealing the shiny hilt of what Lina was sure was a very sharp knife, it reminded Lina of the daydream and all the shiny things in the large room not so long ago. Adaleen saw Lina smiling at her as she picked up the tied-up furs.

"What's got you so happy this morning? Jasper didn't tell you the plan did he?" Lina cocked her head to the side in surprise, she racked her mind to remember some slip of a plan.

"No he didn't say anything, I'm just happy to be doing something other than chores I guess," Lina said thinking carefully as she spoke. Adaleen can tell when lies are being spilled so she chose her words carefully to be sure they were true, though not necessarily the proper answer to the question.

"All right well, let's head out before all the good stuff is gone!" Adaleen twisted on her heels and headed for the exit. Lina was right behind her. They walked out into the morning with the sun working its way high up in the sky. Adaleen put her hand up and checked the sky for clouds.

"Not one sign of cloud, rain season is finally over with." She turned to Lina and handed her the furs. Lina was grateful to help and took them and followed alongside her friend who headed up the street. The walk was pleasant, they had a short way to go and they moved at a leisurely pace. Being an off day for both, they took the time they had earned through their hard work. As they walked, Lina looked at the houses that grew bigger and nicer as she continued on. All the buildings this far out were shabbier than closer into the village. She noted when they started getting bigger, and when they started having multiple chimney stacks. Even the quality of the walls changed from the shabby cheap wood her little hut was made of, to richer, more expensive lumber. Makes sense as lumber was this area's main export. There were only two buildings made of stone in their entire village, they were closest to the market. One was the church, where a bunch of rich town folk collected to praise a god that they apparently believed in. Lina wasn't sure about their god, it seemed he only helped the well off in her opinion. The only other stone building was Crestfallen Manor, where her mother acquired her work. The Lord Renfeild of

Crestfallen Manor was a quiet man. He always had this look of wanting to be someplace else when Lina saw him. Lina never knew why, as he had the finest estate and a beautiful wife and even an annoying heir who constantly reminded everyone, he could do whatever he wanted.

"Where has your mind run off to?" Adaleen asked giving Lina a side-glance as Lina gazed ahead of her thoughtfully.

"I was just wondering why Lord Renfeild always looks so discontent..." she mused with Adaleen looking curiously to see if she had any ideas.

"Oh Lord Renfeild has his secrets just like the rest of us, I assure you. I heard, he doesn't fancy a life with his pretty little wife. I heard he had a thing for the stable boys before the arranged marriage..." She added the last bit in a hush just above a whisper, looking around for eavesdroppers.

"What... no... surely a lord of that standing..."

"Even Lords and Ladies are human young Lina, we all have our desires and only when you allow others to tell you what you are allowed to want do we become tame to societal standard."

"But other boys, I didn't realize that was ever a choice..." She looked confused as she felt Adaleen put her hand on her back.

"It isn't for him, that is why I believe he always looks so discontent..." Adaleen touched her nose with the end of this statement symbolizing Lina was right to question all of this and to have a look of outrage over it.

"When I become queen people will be with whom they want and love not who their parents and peers chose for them," Lina said kicking up dirt and watching it catch in the breeze. Adaleen grabbed hold of Lina's arm softly halting her in place.

"Queens don't get themselves dirty." She wiped some dust from her dress. "We are nearing inner town now; I want you to stay close to me. Take nothing from no one without my permission and do not make eye contact with the salacious woman. If they sense weakness, they will try to pick your pocket or worse try to take you. Understood?"

"Yes, I remember the rules." Lina kind of pouted and pulled the best sorry look she could before asking, "Can we go by the magic stall, and the spice stall? I'd love to see the ribbon store even if we can't get anything!" Lina started bouncing with excitement looking down the street to the market.

"We will go to everything you want, but let's make haste, the square is filling as we speak." And Adaleen smiled as she led the way down the remainder of the road that opened to the square.

The square was a large lot that had stalls and markets set up on all sides. Some were small shabby places with cheap things, and some were large buildings with huge stock of everything you need. From their entrance they stood across from the front of Crestfallen Manor which had a pub, a hotel and a shop of fabrics in front of it. To its immediate left was the church, a large ominous building with a bell that was rang often, though Lina never knew what it was rang for. The sun still hadn't climbed to its highest point and was causing the church to cast a bit of a shadow on Crestfallen Manor, leaving it looking strangely dark and abandoned. Adaleen led Lina by her elbow toward the center of the square where there were a few places to trade furs. After negotiating with a salesman for a few moments she unwrapped the wares and traded all the hides for a decent looking bag of silver. Adaleen turned to Lina as she tucked the bag of silver safely away under a layer of shirts and looked up to her. Then she froze, her eyes looking just past Lina to a shop close by. Lina followed her eyes and saw Berry Renfeild, the son of the lord of Crestfallen Manor standing some paces behind her.

Adaleen, as if not even thinking, grabbed Lina's elbow and dragged her to the opposing corner of the square. With all the people gathering at this point they were mostly out of sight. Adaleen slowed and followed the shadows like a cat until they arrived at a used goods store. It wasn't the nicest in the area and certainly had some questionable display items such as a shrunken head, a dusty bottle of what looked like blood, and some sort of silver crystal liquid in a vile.

"Adaleen, and a friend, what a delight what can I help you with today?" A tiny hunched over old man was standing behind the counter. He could barely be seen over it, but his voice rang out clear and strong. Stronger perhaps than Adaleen was prepared for.

"Hush Arwin, let's deal in the back and keep your voice down." Adaleen rushed with Lina to the side of the counter and behind it ducking under the blankets obscuring the sides to see a caravan that had been hidden by the blankets and booth.

"You know I will not accept stolen goods Adaleen…" the man rasped in a quieter tone now that they were huddled in the back.

"Yea, yea I also know what kind of curses you put on people who lie to you so do me a favor and give me a chance to explain all right." Adaleen threw her hand on her hip and looked at the man with her interrogating stare.

"All right what have you got then?" The old man held out a knotted withered hand that shook slightly with his effort.

Lina noted he didn't look well, as if he were older than the town and time itself. Adaleen handed him the knife which she had tucked away in the folds of her jacket and stood back looking at a jar full of what looked like live beetles. The man ran his hands on the knife and stopped at the crest.

"This isn't stolen?" he asked uncertainly.

"No I won it off that Brat Berry from Crestfallen Manor. You can test it with your powder stuff if you don't believe me, it's mine, fair and square." She tossed her dark braided hair over her shoulder with impatience as the old man hobbled over to the caravan. He seemed to open a drawer from nowhere and procured a little box with dark etchings all over it. He then sat out a cloth, Lina was watching very intently curious as to what he was doing. The man took the box and opened it then set the knife on the cloth. He sprinkled a tiny bit of powder on the knife and the powder would touch the blade then bounce. As Lina watched the man started murmuring words over the blade and the powder started moving as if being controlled. The powder shifted above the knife and created a circle in the middle of the air, suddenly in the circle she saw Adaleen and Lord Berry. They weren't alone but the other figures were unidentifiable. They were shooting arrows at a target… and Berry was very obviously losing. They shot a few and it became obvious Adaleen had won so Berry handed her the knife.

"You won't have this long… I'll get it back soon enough…" Berry said to her while Adaleen raised her head in triumph for having won against the brat.

"Well now, you just try…" She laughed in his face… "Maybe choose to bet on something you're actually good at then."

Suddenly all the powder dropped causing a weird hazy smoke to kick up slightly. The old man coughed, and Lina grabbed her gourd and took the cap off to offer him a sip and dug in her bag to get him some bread and jerky. Taken aback by the kind offer, he accepted and took a long low draw of the water and nibbled the bread never taking his eyes off Lina.

"I told you, it's a royal crested blade, made of silver. And not stolen I won't have less than twelve gold pieces—"

"Excuse me…" Lina cut off Adaleen mid barter. "But was that magic?" Lina asked the man pointing at the knife covered in powder. The man considered his answer carefully before giving it to Lina.

"I dabble in many kind of goods miss, and yes magic is one of them… but that doesn't always mean it's good, now you remember that. You will need it for the journey." Lina looked at Adaleen and saw they were both utterly confused by the statement. What journey? The walk home?

"You want to be clearer on what you mean by that?" Adaleen asked, irritation beginning to show on her face.

"Exactly twenty gold pieces for the knife," said the man randomly with a smile.

"Are you getting on in the head old man, I only asked for twelve…" Adaleen exclaimed, shocked at the jump in price. "I'm not trying to rob you blind; there is no way it's worth that much…"

"You two are worth a lot more to all of us than you have yet to realize." With these last words the man scurried to yet another (non-existent Lina now knew) drawer and fished out a bag of gold. He thrusted it into Adaleen's hand and pushed them towards the exit. The blankets on the ends of the stand slid back into place and Adaleen and Lina stood rooted to the spot for a moment. Confusion gripping them both. Adaleen weighed the bag in her hand and knew it was much too heavy, she opened it and counted out over thirty gold pieces.

"That senile old fart is barking… he overpaid twice I'm gunna give him the extra back. She turned to return the extra gold then gasped and took a step back. Adaleen grabbed Lina's elbow yet again and twisted her and asked…

"Is it just me or is his whole stand and caravan gone right now." And sure enough as Lina rubbed her eyes to double check the entire stand, the blankets all over it, the weird little display, all of it was gone. They stood near the only open empty spot along the wall.

"Magic men never make much sense…" Adaleen said shaking her head and turning again on the spot. "Oh shit."

Adaleen had turned just in time to see Berry walking up with his friends laughing amongst themselves.

"Well, look who we found boys…"

Chapter 3

Adaleen quickly shifted Lina behind her and away from any harm but kept a firm grip as she began to shuffle backwards away from the boys. There were only four of them including Berry but that isn't good odds for two girls. Regardless, Adaleen put herself between Lina and the boys and shuffled to where they could not be trapped, keeping the wall on her left.

"Look at that, come down from your daddy's rich estate to lose some more heirlooms to me now?" Adaleen teased, but Lina knew she was buying time to find them an escape route. She looked over Adaleen's shoulder at the boys. They were basically men, each slightly taller than Adaleen with lean builds. They weren't strong compared to Jacob or as tall, as a matter-of-fact they wouldn't dare say anything if he were there but he wasn't... The three around Berry seemed his caliber if not a bit dim. He usually surrounded himself with the most prosperous kids in town leaving him to be the only one of them who could afford a true education. The three cronies sulked around him attempting to intimidate the girls though Adaleen stood unaverred. Lina accidentally let out a small laugh about this situation. There were four almost grown men failing at intimidating a single woman.

"Ah what's that little Lina, having another dream of being rich and loved." Berry mocked Lina openly pretending to swoon for a prince.

"At least she is fit for royalty, you aren't even fit to be a man." Adaleen spit the words at him threateningly. It is a big risk to come for a person's manhood even if you are a fellow man. Berry furiously lurches forward and attempts to backhand Adaleen; she dodges it with ease, sticks her feet between his and kicks up under his knee. He falls to the ground quickly and she just as quickly grabs Lina's arm and weaves them through the busier and busier square.

"No I'm fine, just get them!" Berry attempts to rally his troops who fail miserably at the upkeep trying to help up their posh boss. Before any of them could register the order, they had gone a quarter of the way down the square and were gaining speed. Weaving through people effortlessly Adaleen attempted to drag Lina through, Lina not as clean with getaways gets a little jostled in the mix but held it together as they made it inside a pub on the outskirts of the square. The door shut behind them and a few patrons raised a pint as a way of hello, Adaleen continued to make her way to the back past the twenty or so tables where she sat them in a corner to catch their breath facing the door.

"I think we lost them," Adaleen said waving down the barmaid.

"Hungry now dear?" said the plump woman who walked up to the table. She was cleaning her hands on her dirty apron, which helped Lina feel better as it was something she did often.

"Uh yea do you have stew and bread? Make it two of each, and I'll have a cider if you got any and just a water, Lina?" Adaleen looked at Lina then nodded at the barmaid to complete the order. "You need to eat, we both do… after all that running around and barely eating breakfast. You need the energy in case they catch back up. We can wait here a while and eat then head back to your place, which should be enough time for Jacob and Jasper to come around if even one comes looking for us, they won't come near us again. I swear I have never seen cowards stand so tall before…" Adaleen shook her head and chuckled to herself.

"Say maybe you shouldn't tell Jacob this happened…" Lina was suddenly worried her brother would be upset.

"I'll have to, he will have to keep an eye on you closer if they decide to put you against them with me… I'd never forgive myself if I didn't say anything and something happened to you." Adaleen reached across the table and took Lina's hand. "We are family, he will understand."

Just then the door to the pub they both entered swung open hard. Lina ducked down in fear they had been found and followed. Adaleen dropped her head low and threw a scarf over her hair until she heard the men talking which was not hard as they were being quite loud.

"Crestfallen village… it should be Crestfallen. There is nothing left to fall!" Followed by loud laughter from the other soldiers who just joined the pub crowd. Seemingly drunk and riding in from somewhere almost fifteen soldiers came in the room hollering asking for ale and drinks. The soldiers were not our normal security we had a couple soldiers in town, but these were soldiers of the king. With nice armor and clean leathers, Adaleen became curious what they were doing here.

Just then the barmaid came back with their food and drinks, she bid them a pardon and ran to get things in order for the soldiers. Adaleen took her scarf and tossed it to Lina, then swept her hand over her head signaling for her to cover her hair. Lina tied the scarf around her covering her hair up and silently watched Adaleen scoping out the crowd. Lina saw Adaleen eyeing two men that had come in with the others but were sitting farther back near them. The group as a whole was pretty loud so overhearing conversation wouldn't be easy. Adaleen put her finger to her lips, then stood and walked to the bar and spoke quickly with the barmaid. Lina couldn't be sure but she thought she saw an exchange of gold between the two. Then Adaleen put on an apron and came back towards the table. She stopped at the table the men were at just before reaching it, and turned as if paying attention to something the barmaid had said. She stood for a moment before turning and asking if the men would like food or drink. They ordered something and she turned to leave walking as slowly as she dared to. Lina watched and ate her stew somehow ravenously after all the events of the day. She sipped at her water and watched Adaleen bring the gentlemen drinks slowly again, then walk away slowly again. This time she stopped at the table next to theirs and slowly started wiping it down. A couple of the soldiers who saw jeered at her but she paid them no mind. Her ears were strained, and her face was fixed in concentration. She then rose quickly and scurried back to the bar. She handed over the apron and gestured for Lina to join her. Lina lapped up the last of her stew, threw her bread in their bag and went to follow Adaleen out the door.

"I thought we had to wait before leaving..."

"I forgot we had to go someplace don't worry it's not in the square." Adaleen took her down an ally she hadn't used before held up her hand before emerging on the streets.

"I have just found out some very interesting things from the chaps at the pub," Adaleen mused with a smile that turned into a grin.

"Was it about why they are here?" Lina wondered aloud to Adaleen who was smiling so big now she was the one practically vibrating from happiness.

"Yes, there is a good reason and a bad reason... but let us only focus on the good." She looked out into the street and checked that the coast was clear for sure before whisking Lina forward into the street then quickly into a shop. Lina barely had a chance to catch her balance before she looked around and was struck breathless. She was in a dress shop. Adaleen had taken her in a dress shop, and it was filled with the most beautiful and elegant looking dresses Lina had ever seen.

"Adaleen why?" Lina looked at Adaleen who was again smiling broader than ever before.

"Because Young Lina, I have just learned that there is going to be a Royal Guest at the spring festival a fortnight from now." Lina stood shocked. She had to be wrong, royals don't come to Crestfallen village not real ones anyway. They pass through, sure, but they never stopped.

"But why... why now I don't understands." Lina looked at Adaleen with nothing but questions. Adaleen took her hand to reassure her.

"You let me worry about the why, You just worry about making sure that whoever this royal is he sees you." She again let a matter-of-fact smile slide on her face. "Excuse me," she suddenly proclaimed loudly as suddenly a male dress maker materialized from apparently nowhere.

"My friend needs a dress for the spring festival in a fortnight... something beautiful... something that says, 'I am and always have been better than this place', and even more important something you are not going to sell to anyone else before the festival."

"Important night mam?" exclaimed the female seamstress who also came from apparently nowhere. She began to hum and take measurements.

"Are you sure this is a good idea?" Lina asked Adaleen as she started feeling fabrics and looking at buttons.

"It's strange really, it's like I haven't ever been more sure. Like it wasn't even my idea but it came from me.

That's probably because it was Jasper's though. Told you I had a surprise, we always planned on you leaving with a new dress. We just didn't know we would have so much for it or that there was a good reason to spend that much oddly enough... You can thank him when we get back. I'm sure they will be hungry, and I got to talk to him and Jacob."

"About the bad news?" Lina suddenly remembered the troops being here wasn't all good.

"Yea but don't you worry I'm sure Jacob will know what it's about or what to do." Adaleen looked at Lina and told her to pay attention to the seamstress.

"Chin up dear," she was saying tapping underneath Lina's chin to hold it up higher for some reason. Lina let go of a giggle that caused Adaleen to start laughing.

"You know, I always thought with your hair you needed softer color like the blue dress but maybe you should wear something bold..."

"You two do have money right..." The dress maker stood back putting a hand on his hip judging the clothing of Lina and Adaleen.

"Nuff to shut the likes of you up... and we want the nice material don't be cutting corners or I'll be cutting fingers ya hear me..." Adaleen reached in her pocket and pulled out about six gold coins. The shopkeeper jumped on the spot and mentioned some bold colors in silk in the back and hurried to get them for her.

A few hours later, Adaleen and Lina left the shop with a slightly lighter purse than when they entered. The dress was being made from scratch and Lina would have to return in three days' time to do a fitting. Adaleen promised to go with her as they made their way down the street towards Lina's home. She also assured her Jasper was to fill Jacob in on the dress surprise while they were out so he wouldn't think Lina had accepted a gift of stolen it.

"Did they say who the royal guest would be? Is he staying in the hotel?" Lina asked trying to get as much info out of her tight-lipped friend as she could.

"They didn't say much just that he was staying in the manor so they would be posted there and that he was around Berry's age. No clarification on title or family which could be a bummer." Adaleen saw disappointment on Lina's face.

"What's wrong Lina this is a good thing..." Adaleen grabbed her arm affectionately trying to decipher the worry in her friend's face.

"It's just, Berry doesn't like me... He makes fun of me—if he spends time with the person, he is sure to not like me either..." Lina couldn't meet her eyes as she explained her worry. But shut them up when she heard Adaleen laughing at her statement.

"Impossible, Berry is a self-centered worm who only cares about his title and getting what he wants, any real royal would see right through him if they deserved to be royal at all. Not to mention anyone who doesn't like you is a mule's ass..." Adaleen shook with laughter at the thought of Lina being unappealing to anyone. Adaleen has watched Lina for years and has seen her become more and more beautiful inside and out the entire time. She suddenly remembered seeing a dirty little girl sitting soaking wet at a grave.

"Put it out of your mind for now, we will have to get ready for the festival and we have yet to dump the bad news on your brother along with informing him about poor old Berry who will surely cower into shadows when he sees him next, royal friend or no…" Adaleen lead the way back down the streets away from the square and the noise. The walk seemed so short on the way back they barely noticed when they got there as Lina almost passed her own home.

Lina turned to go in with Adaleen and saw smoke in the chimney and mused that the boys must have beat them back.

"Hey guys," they both rang out together as they walked in the hovel, while setting down their various bags scarves and jackets. No answer… Lina went and checked out back and saw no sign of the guys returning.

"Lina come quickly…" Adaleen had rushed behind her from the hallway. Lina immediately terrified ran toward her and her mother's room, she saw her before she got to the door. Laying on the ground next to a pile of sick was her mother. She had burns up and down her arms and, on her face, and neck. Her hair was singed and every breath she took looked painful. Lina took a step back seeing the raw blisters all over her mother's fair skin. Her eyes welled up with tears as she questioned what could have happened. She went to try to help her onto the bed but she screamed out in so much pain Lina thought she could feel it too. Then Lina was screaming, screaming for help and crying. Holding onto her mother and begging for anybody to please get some help.

"I... I gotta find the boys I'll be right back, try to get her to drink some water!" And, in a flash, Adaleen had run from the room, thundered down the hallway and booked it off in the direction of the valley screaming for Jasper and Jacob with every spare breath she could muster.

"Okay... okay... water, I'm gunna get you some water Mom..." Lina jumped up from her useless position and ran to the other room for a cup of water. She checked all the buckets, and they were empty then she remembered her gourd she had sat on the table when she came in. She ran to it thinking it should be almost empty after the little man all but drained it, but sure enough it was basically full. She thought for a second about this, then decided it didn't matter and ran back to her mother again. She sat behind her mother and tried to lift her head up to get her to drink. Her mother's eyes were fluttering open and closed periodically like she was passing out. Lina wondered if her medicine did this... is it possible she fell in the fire herself? But how could she have carried herself back here like this?

"It's okay Ma it's just me, I need you to drink some water okay." Lina cradled her mother's head like a baby and put the water to her mouth over and over, cooing softly that it would be all right and Adaleen would be back with

Jacob any moment. Once her mother would no longer drink, she set the water down and hummed to her to try and comfort her.

"Lina..." She heard her brother calling from the distance she knew Adaleen must have reached them. It calmed her heart knowing he was coming, that she wasn't in this alone. She closed her eyes and stopped humming. She listened very intently for him, she knew he could probably race a horse and win if his mother or her needed him. She began to hear the heavy footfalls softly at first. Then louder as Jacob beelined for the house and his small broken family.

"Lina I'm here." He was in the home and down the hall in less than a second but gasped when he entered the room and saw his mother.

"She... she said she got burned but..." Jacob looked at his sister with tears in his eyes. What were they going to do. They couldn't afford the kind of things that could fix this...

"We have to get her clothes off to see how bad it is... Jasper mentioned gathering something to help with cleaning the wounds." Jacob took his sharpest knife off his waist and kneeled down next to his sister.

"Jacob I'm sorry but I don't know if I can..." Lina looked desperately at her brother, she had a terribly weak stomach when it came to things like blood. She already had a pallor to her skin and a glazed look in her eye. This is why Lina couldn't hunt.

"Why don't you make us some supper to help, Mom will need to eat after this, I'll have to clean the wounds and dress them... I just hope they aren't too deep... Do you know what happened?" Jacob looked to his sister hoping for some explanation.

"No, we came home, and she was like this..." Lina explained thinking back to the exact moment she got there. "We saw the smoke in the chimney and thought you got back first."

"All right go get some air, I'm gunna get her cleaned up; when the twins get back send them to the room, please." With that Jacob stood up. "We will need more water if you could?"

"Yes, I'll go fetch it right now..." And Lina turned to leave the room. She noticed for the first time that there was a specific smell stuck in her nose. She tried not to think of it being the smell of her mother being cooked. She grabbed the empty water pails and went to go to the front door when she noticed something. The plate of breakfast she left out for her mom was practically licked clean... strange, her mom never ate that much, especially when she was on meds. She decided to think about it later as right now her mother and brother desperately needed her.

Lina ran down the street and a half away to the well and filled her buckets as quickly as she could. It seemed to take forever for her to heave them back up the well. She finally collected the second bucket and turned to trudge back as quickly as she could. She saw a neighbor outside heading home watch her curiously as she struggled to move faster. When she was outside her home, Jasper came out and grabbed a bucket. He and Lina hurried inside where he, without a word, walked to the back with some plants. Lina started trying to rouse the fire as her mother's screams of agony filled every dark corner of the little cabin. Lina doubled down and worked harder. She went outside to grab some meat and found a fowl freshly plucked and gutted waiting for her. She grabbed the goose and then took a few deep breaths. Even here she could hear her mother, She kept breathing, holding the bird opened her eyes. She looked to the sky and she started feeling tears roll towards her eyes. She wanted to be an adult and wanted to hold back, but it was too much. She stared at the sky silently while tears streamed down her face, while she listened to her mother's continued screaming from pain. She looked at the door to her home and cursed as she walked back inside the cabin to begin dinner.

About fifteen minutes into cooking, Adaleen finally showed up, but she wasn't alone. With her was a woman with long, coarse curly hair, and the darkest skin Lina had ever seen. She had seen the woman before, she recognized the bones in her hair and jewelry along with the patchy dirty dress. Adaleen had brought the forest's witch.

"Uh, Adaleen. What are you doing?" Lina asked curiously looking at the woman.

"I saw those burns Lina, we need all the help we can get. Celeste here owes me a favor after I helped her out a while back, so she is willing." Adaleen nodded and started walking down the hallway followed closely by her silent friend, Celeste. Lina didn't know what Jacob would make of this but didn't imagine he had a lot of fight in him after what she had been hearing. She didn't hear any protest if he had any and not long after Celeste and Adaleen entered the room the screaming finally stopped. Lina finally felt the tight clench in her gut she hadn't even known was there, release. She busied herself with dinner and making potatoes and soup to go with the roast bird she had on a spit in the fire. Jasper and Adaleen came out first and explained what was happening. Apparently, Celeste used some powdered herb to cool her blood down and put her to sleep. Then she was rubbing a salve on the burns. Apparently, she would need this often. Lina heard every word they said but couldn't absorb any of the information. Suddenly, Jasper turned to them both and asked exactly what happened when they got home. They explained the events, and Lina ventured as far as to tell them about the clean plate which seemed unnatural.

"There were at least two to three eggs and two to three sausages on that plate when we left... she couldn't have eaten that, could she?" Adaleen thinking back to when they left.

"No she couldn't." Jacob had entered the room looking glum, Celeste behind him. Celeste handed Jacob a jar filled with a thick white substance and began to walk through the room. As she approached where Lina sat, she stopped and suddenly looked in awe, she stooped and bowed to her and lightly grazed her foot with her hand before quickly standing and walking through the door and out the back of the cabin.

"Well that was weird... even for her..." said Adaleen a little shocked. Lina cracked a smile, the first smile since she got home.

"She said we could have this..." Jacob said questioningly holding out the jar.

"I swear by that stuff Jacob, I kid you not, burnt myself building a fire one night, got myself real bad. Used some of Celeste's ointment and it was cleared up in like two days." Jasper started to recount.

"Were you burned that bad though?" asked Jacob sincerely looking doubtful.

"Uh, not actually but still it's got to be better than nothing. I mean she's got the magic and all..." Jasper just ended his statement when he saw the look on his sister's face. "What is it?"

"Well... I had a little bad news to deliver before all this happened and I'm not sure if I should just wait on it." Adaleen looked uncomfortable while Lina checked on dinner and Jacob who looked very tired but gave her his attention.

"Well let's have it then..." Jasper pushed his sister just a bit.

"First off, when we went to the market, we ran into Berry who started threatening me and took a swipe at me... but we got away..." she added seeing the looks on both boys' faces. "The real problem was the other part. We saw the king's soldiers in town and I was able to eavesdrop why they are here. Turns out a royal is coming to town… to distract everyone from the rebellion closing in on our borders…"

"Wait what…" Jacob's eyes flashed over and got wide. "The rebellion is supposed to be hundreds of miles from here, when, how, did it get so close?"

"Well that's the thing… They set up a camp a way out of town apparently… keeping an eye on us so to speak but… With the way things are going we should be safe according to guy who was talkin' about it anyway." Adaleen had an unconvinced look on her face.

"Ya know, I don't even know for sure what they are rebelling…" said Jasper looking to Jacob for some wisdom.

"Taxes, land, hierarchy, school systems, all of it really…" Jacob listed things off using his fingers to count them. "At least from what I have heard…" he added a bit mysteriously.

"Either way we have a fortnight till the festival, and we should make sure we make a decent amount of sales. Meat sells for way more around feasts. If we all hunt and Lina scavenges herbs and veggies, we will make a killing and be able to feast ourselves!" Adaleen was still set on the idea of going to the festival. Lina even though she knew she had a stunning dress wasn't sure with her mother's condition that it would be appropriate.

"Jacob shouldn't…"

"You're going... remember what we talked about Lina. This could be good—and I will be there with you the whole time," Jacob told her firmly.

"Great, so we will check on the dress in a few days and ... Lina your bird is burning..."

Lina twisted around and grabbed the towel and the spit and tried to get the bird out of the fire...

"Ouch!" The grease slid down and splattered her hand. She grabbed the potatoes and soup and set everything up then remembered the bread in her bag and grabbed that too.

As Lina sat down with everyone else her brother handed her the cream left by Celeste.

"For your hand..." Jacob said with an unbelieving chuckle.

"Jasper it doesn't have anything weird in it, does it?" She looked at him and he scoffed.

"She lives way too close to the cemetery for me to feel comfortable saying that..." replied Jasper earnestly while spearing a roasted potato and taking a wing from the goose.

"I'll live I think," said Lina as she passed the jar back to her brother who was already eating. The room grew quiet as they all sat around eating, famished from the day and exhausted for the morrow already. The twins left shortly after, and Jacob and Lina were alone.

"Lina, do you think this was an accident?" Jacob asked her...

"I don't know…" Lina answered honestly thinking of the odd little man and what he said she looked her brother in the eyes. "But if it wasn't I have a feeling we will find out…"

Chapter 4

The next five days were a blur of taking care of their mother and stocking up on merchandise for the big festival. Lina and Jacob refused to leave their mother alone until they found out what happened to her when they were gone, so Jasper and Adaleen would help out by sitting with Olive when they both had to busy themselves keeping things going. With the sales being made to Crestfallen Manor, Jacob was able to buy three more chickens, and with Jasper and Adaleen's continued help they have been pulling in more meat than ever. They portioned everything so they could maximize their profits, but all stay well-fed, which was made easier with the extra hands to help.

On the sixth morning when she woke up, Lina stretched on the ground as she had been letting her mother sleep on the whole bed while she healed. She rose very slowly, rubbing her eyes, then her back. The floor was not very giving when seeking comfort at night. Lina rose her arms over her head and yawned turning her head from the left to the right. She opened her eyes and looked to the bed where her mother... was gone. Lina jumped up in a panic and began ruffling the raggedy blankets as if she were hiding in them.

"Mother, Mother!" She yelled the second word with urgency as she dived under the bed—surely, she had just fallen off in the night. Lina's eyes adjusted as she took in the shapes of blankets and nothing. Her mother was gone…

Lina rose from the ground dashed to the door in only a few steps and opened it to find Jacob standing outside the other room looking tired and ruffled but somehow also alert.

"What's wrong what's happened with Mother?" he asked crossing the hall to the room and pushing past Lina.

"What…" He moved into the room while Lina stood back and he too began ruffling the blankets, though he gave up quickly and rose to run to the hallway and down to the kitchen. There Jacob began to look around, it was still pretty dark, but nothing was out of place from the night before other than their mother being gone. No food had been moved or touched, no bags had been taken or anything.

"I thought maybe she woke up feeling… where did she go? Did you hear anything Lina?" Jacob looked at his sister desperately trying to make sense of his groggy thoughts that were trying to draw some answer from her.

"I heard nothing, I slept on the floor right next to her. Could she have left?" Lina asked confusion gripping her as she considered the other possibilities, but no one could have snuck in, she would have heard… Jacob just looked thoughtful. He stood in the kitchen staring off for a while then walked out the back door. he came back with a cup of beans to make coffee and Lina absent-mindedly went to getting the fire going and crushing the beans. Jacob looked worried.

"There are no tracks leaving that look new..." he told Lina with his head hung. He sat at the table, and they were both silent. The only sound for a while was the water in the pot getting hot and the fire crackling.

Knock, knock. Just as Lina was pulling the coffee off the hearth Jasper poked his head at the door. He immediately felt the temperature of the room as Adaleen pushed the door open.

"Everything all right?" Adaleen asked eyeing Jacob wearily.

"I'm going to get the eggs for breakfast." Lina attempted to bolt not wanting to reface the reality that their mother was gone. She had held it together so far and she wanted to try to continue to. Nobody stopped her as she grabbed her apron and hastily left the room. She walked to the chicken coop slowly and didn't even realize when she picked up the feed and moved through the gate. She was thinking about her mother and how she could have left without a word or goodbye. She began spreading the feed to rouse the chickens up and started collecting the eggs. She had eight today which was better than lately. She carefully tucked the eggs in her apron and walked out of the coop reaching the gate and headed to the smoke shack. She walked in and saw a stack of bacon. sliced up and ready to cook. She grabbed it and a jar of fat. She was running low inside. She walked back to the door and listened to make sure story time was over. Once she heard the talking stop she went in and started setting down the food. She stoked the fire and added her grate to cook on then set to work with the eggs and bacon. A silence hung in the room while she worked with the occasional sip of some coffee. Lina's cooking filled the room with the delicious scent of bacon and a sizzling sound that broke some of the silence finally.

"Well I think she left on her own accord, just doesn't make sense for her to be taken with Lina sleeping right there..." Jasper finally said to further break the silence.

"My thoughts exactly, nothing is gone though, where could she have gone... how could she get there?" Jacob answered, shrugging and looking defeated.

"Look, Olive has lived here forever, she probably came to and went to see some friend or something..." Adaleen said trying to sound hopeful but not quite selling it with her tone and eyes.

"Should I report her missing?" Jacob said aloud to no one in particular.

"You can try but you will be pressed to find someone who actually cares, she was hooked on medicine and had all but removed herself from the village eye, on top of that her contributions to the people were very little..."Adaleen told Jacob holding his eyes to ensure he understood what she was saying. More or less her disappearance would be written off as a drug-related issue. The authorities would not look for her or answers after talking to the town doctor.

"We can't just do nothing…" Jacob looked desperately at Adaleen and Jasper, who, in turn, looked to each other.

Lina continued to cook and keep herself busy piling up the bacon and eggs on one plate and cutting a loaf of slightly old bread. She pretended to be busy but really, she was listening intently on what they might do. She was just as curious about this situation as so many others. The fact is this is not the first time a person had disappeared right around her, She vaguely thought of the market and the magic man.

"We won't," Adaleen started as Lina carried the plate of food over and everyone thanked her.

"Me and Jasper will ask around and listen in on what we can to see if anything else was amiss last night. We haven't been to the square in a while so we will take a look and listen there. Can you handle checking the traps and solo hunting today?"

Adaleen started quickly making plans to get as much information as they could. She didn't notice Lina watching her as she named off the best pubs to get information from and who to shake down for confidential notes in town. Lina nibbled at some eggs while the boys began to dive in. Jasper made some kind of open egg and bacon sandwich and started devouring it while Jacob ate mostly bacon to no doubt give him some strength.

Once Adaleen had finished, she took a piece of bacon and a bit of eggs and turned to Lina.

"Your dress is almost done. I had them make a few last-minute alterations. Just another nice little surprise for you."

The dress? The festival, Lina had so much on her mind at the moment that she had completely forgotten.

"Wait…" Jacob suddenly put his hand up to Adaleen looking intensely at her. "If we find or hear anything about our mother being taken or hurt… I think it's best that Lina sits the festival out just to be safe," Jacob added the last words to Adaleen who clearly had a rebuttal at her lips. Adaleen slumped back and crossed her arms over her chest in defeat. She knew he was right, they had to be sure she was safe and that there wasn't some sort of target out there.

"Lina you probably shouldn't be going out on your own, when you aren't here, maybe Adaleen can accompany you to gather and pick up your dress just for the next while or until we learn you are for sure safe." Jacob added this, and Lina knew she was going to have to start learning to protect herself.

"Okay," Lina said, making a mental note to ask Adaleen to show her some defense in their time together. She never wanted to be helpless and hates the idea of being a burden. Breakfast as usual never came to the table this morning, however. There was a glum quiet to everything said and everyone was more mindful than usual. The twins didn't bicker at all and Jacob kept looking at Lina like he had lost her too. After eating, the twins bid farewell to go see what they could find out from the village folk and promised to return later with any and all news. Jacob looked at Lina as she cleaned up from breakfast and asked if she wanted company foraging and gathering today. Lina tried not to be offended he didn't want to leave her alone and knew they need not hunt today if he didn't want to so she asked if he remembered the clearing in the woods their father took them to when they were little. It was too deep in the forest for Lina to venture to alone, but she knew at this time of year there would be a lot of ripe mushrooms and berries she could pick. They hadn't had wild berries in a really long time. Jacob agreed to take her there once she was ready.

An hour or so later, Jacob and Lina set off into the back of the house to go to the clearing she hadn't visited in a few years. She had a bag to carry mushrooms and a basket for any ripe berries. The forest is thinner near town where a lot has been cut down and used for lumber, but the trees get denser quickly and the light becomes somewhat obscured by the canopy. The smell of moist dirt and moss meets her nose, and she takes a big breath in. She looks up and sees mismatched trees fighting to be the tallest. A lot of them are huge but some of them are smaller or grow at strange angles, half dying covered in fungi and moss. Jacob walks with purpose because he knows exactly where he is going. It's about a two-hour walk to the clearing. He brought his bag, a bow and quiver, a knife, and a larger blade in case of predators. They also carried their gourd of water and occasionally stopped and took turns taking a drink, resting on a tree trunk or a large outward growing root.

By the time they reached the clearing it was getting close to midday. Lina looked at the grass that was meant to grow up to her knees, it was still ankle-length and patchy. She looked across the way at all the bushes and trees filled with growing fruits that weren't in season yet. She looked towards the little pond that ended a stream that had separated from the river and the animals on either side enjoying a refreshing drink. She looked down and immediately noticed mushrooms hiding in the tree line in the shade growing on fallen logs and branches that were dead and beginning to decay. Lina smiled and felt free of all the issues she had had for a moment while she closed her eyes and breathed in the fresh air.

"We are here," Jacob stated with a smile. He watched as the animals' ears tweaked in our direction followed by them running for the cover of the trees. Lina, who's feet were killing her, as she was not used to such a long walk through the forest, walked out on the semi-flat ground and laid down. She hadn't realized she was this tired.

"If your gunna fall asleep use some shade or you will regret it soon…" Jacob told her taking steps to the edge of the forest and looking for a long stick. He picked up multiple and threw them back down after looking at the length and checking the buoyancy… then he started cutting a few down until he found one that apparently suited him. Lina propped herself up on her arms and watched as he grabbed a long string out of his bag with a hook tied to one end and a jar of what she assumed was bait. He then hacked away all the little branches on his new fishing pole and tied them on the string. Lina rose and dusted off her dress as she followed Jacob towards the pond. She broke off before he went to find a good spot to sit and went towards the berry bushes. There were many that weren't ripe yet but some had begun falling away from the bushes, so she knew she could scavenge up something. Lina started diving into the bushes to see past what the animals had eaten and found that many berries were ripe on the inside. She began collecting them and kept at it till her basket was almost full. Jacob passed behind her and she looked to see he had already caught multiple fish. He looked back at her and laughed at her awe.

"It's the bait, rancid meat brings them right to me for some reason..."He held up a rope with no less than three decently sized fish on it some still flopping hoping to escape. "Not as fun as bowing rabbits and deer though," Jacob added matter-of-factly as he started digging a little side pool to stash them in until Jacob and Lina leave. Lina decided to switch to foraging mushrooms but sampled a few berries and offered some to Jacob first. He ate a few and told her he would start a fire and cook up a fish for lunch. Lina moved to the edge of the clearing and began hunting mushrooms for her bag. She was finding a lot without having to move out of sight of her brother but got a little lost in checking for poisonous mushrooms. Lina went just past the tree line to check an old stump with plenty fungi and stooped down to look closer. She grabbed a few mushrooms that were mature and turned around to find herself in a very different forest. Lina saw that the clearing she was used to was gone, but another clearing sat in her wake. Confused, she stepped forward and felt a long dress drape behind her. Then she saw a man, A tall handsome man with dark hair and a bow trained right on her. Lina jumped at the scene and turned to run away only to trip on the log she had just harvested mushrooms from.

Lina picked herself up and was confused but had very little time to deal with that as Jacob walked over demanding to know if she was just daydreaming. Lina lied for the first time she could remember.

"No Jacob I just got confused because of everything that has been going on, I swear, I'm right here with you getting food together..." Lina pleaded with her brother to believe her. Jacob sighed and his eyes dropped, his hand reached to his brow, and he considered her words carefully.

"All right, as long as you weren't daydreaming or making believe, I need you to have your wits about you now Lina. This is no longer about growing up, it's about keeping you safe." Jacob took his sister's hand and led her back to where he had built a small fire and spit to cook some fish.

They ate their fill at midday and lay about by the water for a while, dipping their feet in, forgetting about their worries. They packed up and left not too long after to make sure they had plenty of light to get back home. On the walk back Jacob took his bow out and occasionally stopped to listen for birds or deer. He was able to catch six fish plus what they ate and gutted them before they left.

Lina thought his skills as a hunter were getting closer to those of their father's. He took down a crow and a couple squirrels as they walked. They would stop after he collected his trophies, and he would quickly clean the animals and gut them with ease.

When they arrived back home, it was normal in the backyard. The hens were clucking, and the smoke shack had a steady stream coming from it. Jacob's workbench remained untouched. He passed all of this and walked in front of Lina to go inside first. Their home had an eerily silence they were not used to. The fire had gone almost all the way out, but everything was as it had been. Lina went to tend the fire and asked her brother to grab a couple of logs.

"Me and Jasper might have to chop some up soon, our dry reserves are getting low," he mentioned as he left the room for Lina to build the fire up. Before leaving he cut four of the fish off the line and set them on the table. Lina added kindling to the fire and then a log trying not to think about how they didn't need a fifth plate… She then grabbed her basket and tied it up with the drying herbs. She took her mushroom bag and put it down by the foraged vegetables she had stored. Jacob brought in some wood and checked the water pails. He grabbed them to be filled and left out the front door. When he returned, Lina was prepping the fire for cooking and getting out all her ingredients to make fish and vegetables. He told her he was going to prep the meat that he had just gathered and get some smoking and salted. He left the room and the quiet ushered itself in. Lina was just beginning to hope Jasper and Adaleen would be along soon when Jasper knocked on the door.

"Is Jacob back too?" Jasper asked pushing the door open. "We weren't sure where you two had gone honestly..." He scratched the back of his head and made his way to the small table and chairs where Lina prepped the fish.

"We went to a clearing so Jacob could fish while I foraged," Lina told him absent-mindedly rubbing the fish with fat and seasonings. She couldn't get the bones out so she only ever cut it open and seasoned it cooking it with the skin and bones. "It's kind of deep in the forest you would have to ask him how to get there, we used to go with dad..." she trailed off not wanting to think about her father or mother.

"I wonder if Adaleen knows where it is... She went to talk to Celeste after we listened in through town. She thinks we should try at night as that's when most nefarious plans get discussed and carried out, " Jasper told Lina then looked at her a bit alarmed. "But don't you worry about that we will talk to Jacob tonight," he hastily added to try and keep Lina from worrying or thinking about what could have happened. It frustrated her when they treated her this way, like she was only to be an adult when it suited them. While she considered the lack of information that she seemed to receive, she felt a terrible burning sensation in her stomach. She put her hand on her gut and sat down feeling the pain grow.

"Jacob is out back if you need to talk to him," Adaleen told Jasper trying to hide her sudden discomfort. Jasper wasn't fooled. He looked at the grip she had on herself and the pain she was trying to hide and sighed.

"Well I'll have a go at his ear in a moment then. Don't you worry Lina, Adaleen will talk to you soon about that pain you're feeling. She told me to keep an eye out, but she has been waiting."

With that cryptic message, Jasper made for the backdoor as Lina tried to work out what he said. Adaleen would know was all she could pull from it. She went back to setting the grate in the fireplace and turned around to grab the fish when suddenly she was on all fours. The pain in her lower abdomen intensified and she felt something warm trickle down her leg. Lina felt scared, She suddenly thought about how her mother must have felt. She was taken and still in pain, Lina felt the vision around her going dark. She attempted to stand only to fall forward towards the table where she reached out to grab a chair. The pain in her abdomen reared again and she fell forward hitting her head on the table, then everything went dark.

Lina woke up in a dark room with a cold cloth on her head and a warm cloth on her tummy. She realized pretty quickly that she was lying in the bed and smelled the fish she had prepared. She wondered how long she had been out. She reached up and touched her head where a small knot was growing on the right side. She remembered hitting her head. Lina went to sit up and heard someone coming down the hallway followed by a soft knock.

"Feeling better?" Adaleen inquired opening the door just a bit to see if Lina was up.

"Yea I hit my head..." Lina told her, feeling silly. She was embarrassed by the whole situation and didn't know exactly what to say. Adaleen entered the room and closed the door behind her.

"We have much to talk about Lina. It seems you have left childhood and have become a woman fully ... Do you know what this means?" Adaleen looked at Lina nervously not sure if anyone had ever discussed this bit of being a woman to her. Lina remembered the pain she felt in her stomach and feeling something warm on her thigh. She lifted her dress and saw her legs had the remnants of smeared blood on them. Adaleen went to the foot of the bed and grabbed the wash basin.

"You will need to clean it up, when you make in the woods you will need to bury it very deep, so nothing smells it..." She set the basin down at Lina's feet and brushed a hand through her hair.

"Being a woman means bleeding as sure as the moon will become full, it will be your monthly burden just like it is with the rest of us, and it comes at a price. You are now of marrying age, mind, and body, you will need to protect your body just as well as your mind against those who would see it and destroy it. You must be cautious of men from now on and not let them press you as a woman. I have something for you..."

Adaleen set down the bag that was draped around her shoulder and pulled out a couple of things. One was bits of fabric attached to a string. the other was a knife and the other was a waist a sheath.

She explained the bits of fabric and how to use them to keep from making a mess of her dresses and such. Then Adaleen stressed the importance of proper disposal again to make sure she understood predators can smell blood. Then she picked up the knife and sheath.

"Hold out your hand." Lina did as she was told, and Adaleen turned Lina's hand over in hers for a moment "Isn't this the one you burned last week; did you use some of Celeste's salve?" Adaleen asked curiously.

"Yes, no salve, but it healed quickly must not have been as bad as it looked," Lina answered with a shrug.

"Well," Adaleen said putting the hilt of the knife in Lina's hand. "I think it's time you start carrying a knife. I already talked to Jacob, and he agrees; a little protection couldn't hurt things for the time being. I can show you how to wield it properly for defense, it shouldn't be hard as I see you cut things up in the kitchen without a problem. But this means you no longer go anywhere alone without this sheath and this knife; however you want them on you."

"Okay. Why do I have to do this now that I'm a woman?" Lina asked not sure how the two things correlate.

"Has Jacob talked to you about what a wife is to do for a husband?" Adaleen asked looking a little uncomfortable.

"I mean housework cooking and cleaning..." Lina began to think but didn't know what else she could mean.

"No I mean procuring a child as a wife. There is a... thing that people have to do. Problem is, you don't want to do that thing with the wrong guy... ya know what... I should ask Jacob how much he wants you to know really, I'm not the one who should be telling you this." Adaleen stood looking a bit red and slightly ruffled and walked towards the door. "Dinner is done by the way, after you get all cleaned up, we saved a plate for you, you did excellent seasoning and preparing as always."

Adaleen gave Lina a wink and left the room. Lina lifted her dress off her and looked at her stomach, no bruises or burns. She grabbed the rag in the washbasin and cleaned herself up as best she could. She put on the makeshift undergarment that Adaleen had given her, glad that she had something to keep things at bay. She suddenly regretted not asking how much bleeding there would be and made a mental note to ask Adaleen later. She threw an unsoiled dress over her head. She hadn't gone to do laundry since the last time her mom went to the manor, which was ages ago, and decided tomorrow she would make the trip. She opened the door and headed to the small room where Jasper, Jacob and Adaleen were sitting in. She saw a plate of food next to the empty chair and went and sat.

"If you guys really want to go take another listen at the square you can but it's up to you. I'm starting to think with all the weird stuff we have heard that something is going on," Jacob said to the twins as they nurse whatever they are drinking in their cups.

"It's worth a shot. It would be a shame if we didn't try and missed something," Jasper told Jacob setting his cup down. "Plus I could go for a drink a bit stronger." He smiled at his sister who grimaced at him.

"Can you not take anything seriously, we go in, we scope things out quietly and fish for information from anyone who looks new or sketchy." Adaleen told Jasper clearly annoyed.

"It's nighttime and the festival is coming, Everyone is going to be new or sketchy…" Jasper attempted to rationalize. Lina was set to believe him as the festival grows closer people from the outskirts of the kingdom start driving in whatever they've to offer and sell. Farmers, hunters, toy makers, entertainers, all come to make a buck and enjoy the festivities. The spring festival is big here in Crestfallen village, it symbolizes the start of a good year and people all over want to attend. The twins began to argue as Lina finished her food. They got up and bid farewells with a promise to return in the morning, and left. Jacob and Lina were both beat for the day and Lina noticed Jacob didn't seem to want to meet her eye for some reason, so she set the dishes to the side drank a glass of water and bid him goodnight. She was sleeping in the bed tonight; she wondered if, wherever her mother was, she was dreaming of her. She closed her eyes and hugged herself as a tear slid out and hoped that her mother was okay.

Chapter 5

The days leading up to the festival were a blur of chores and quiet house duties. Still, there lingered the occasional silence from all the recent events, but with the festival coming, Jasper and Adaleen wouldn't let it stand for too long. They would boast and joke about the music and people and competitions. They would get going, dancing in the kitchen and acting out the plays with their own words, Lina swore she even saw Jacob smiling a few times. Adaleen would reassure Lina that she would be the most beautiful girl at the festival with the dress they had gotten. The day before the festival, they went to pick up the dress.

"We will have to give you a proper bath tomorrow and try to braid your hair up nice. You were right to pick that material, it suits you." Adaleen started fussing over Lina's long yellow hair a moment then looped her arm with hers as they walked.

"Did you ever find out who the royal is?" Lina asked hoping it was someone noteworthy. Adaleen looked away thoughtfully and turned back to Lina with a smirk.

"I think it's best you find out when you get there," she told Lina mysteriously. They traveled down the streets to the dress shop together, laughing and talking about the festival. Lina remembered there being all kinds of booths and foods and men in costumes acting out scenes, the pubs would be full and at night there is fire and dancing. Everyone in town goes dressed in their best and the square fills until the front of the manor opens for the bonfire. Crestfallen Manor always hosts the bonfire behind the building with enough room in the giant empty space for all the people. Lina was sure the guests would be up at the manor on the brick outlook with the rest of the royals at first. But Berry liked to roam down and harass citizens, so he might follow him down there.

They arrived at the dress shop and walked in. Lina had been here three times now and was still in awe of all the beautiful fabrics when she entered. Adaleen went to the back of the store and a man came out with a dress. Money had already been exchanged but she tipped him a single gold nugget. A large box was placed on the table and Adaleen picked it up and turned to leave.

"How much did that cost you for all of it?" Lina asked wondering how she would ever be able to repay her.

"Nothing I can't make again, so don't worry about it," Adaleen said stubbornly looking at Lina like a kid sister holding the box one handed so she can brush her hair out of her face. "Your cheeks are more flushed lately, it looks good." Adaleen noted as she re-established her grip on the box and went to back out the door.

"I have been feeling different lately," Lina admitted thinking of the random aches and pains she occasionally felt in her lower tummy, in her chest. Her small breasts were beginning to swell and shape, and her hips seemed wider somehow. She hadn't noticed any of the changes happening, but it was no secret her body was different.

"It will all adjust to where it need to be in time, till then I wouldn't worry too much," Adaleen said, surely Lina could trust what Adaleen said. She thought to a few years back when Adaleen's body had started changing. She used to be skinny and awkward, now she had curves she craftily concealed under her clothing. Lina looked at the box and felt a bit nervous for the first time ever. Tomorrow, tomorrow, she would be facing her first royal. She smiled to herself, feeling grateful for having such good friends, having such people who believe in her.

"I would assume most women are going to be flocking to the royal so we will have to take a moment and find the right opportunity," Adaleen started plotting next to Lina aloud but Lina wasn't listening. She was imagining what he would look like and how he would sound. He was just barely older than her so that was perfect, she got a giddy feeling glancing at the box realizing she had a real chance.

"It's not as if we can for sure get you completely alone... oh and can you do the dancing royals do? Well it's no matter I don't know how and Jasper and Jacob have four left feet as if that's possible..." Adaleen kept planning the whole way back to the cabin. By the time they arrived, she had such a big smile on her face it was incredible she was able to talk. They walked in and set the box on the table. Lina went to stoke the fire into life which had started to smolder.

"I'd say as long as we make sure you look your best you have just as much a chance as anyone to get noticed, better actually, compared to the cows in this town you're practically a sure fire," Adaleen added and started listing off the girls in town and their issues.

"I mean Amanda has that pig nose thing and Riana's ears stick out so far, she might hear this, and Marisol has that lip…" She kept going until the smile on Lina's face had broken into fits of laughter. Adaleen knew how the girls in town treated Lina, and why she never made any friends.

"They're just jealous of you, and you don't need them you have me and Jasper." She would always tell a crying Lina after being teased by the kids in town.

A moment later, Jasper and Jacob entered the room. After finding no information about their mother from the village people, Adaleen and Jasper started sticking around to help hunt and protect Lina simultaneously. Adaleen had been sleeping in the bed with Lina, she always passed out over the covers and snored a little but Lina didn't mind. She preferred it to sleeping alone.

"You wouldn't believe the haul we got today if we didn't have the proof. No less than eight rabbits, five geese, two deer and." Jasper drummed on the wall for dramatic effect. "We bagged a turkey. haven't seen one of those around in… years actually." He counted back on his fingers thoughtfully for a moment.

"Turkeys go for a lot around festivals, in the morning I'm going to take it to Crestfallen Manor and see if they were able to procure one yet... if not that will be gold pieces..." Jacob added with a smile. He grabbed a grubby little cup and thrust it in the water. "We also have enough wood till probably autumn, thanks to Jasper." He held his cup up to Jasper in thanks.

"Oh I have to either work myself out or drink to sleep..." Jasper said sheepishly not meeting anyone's eyes.

"He really does, never seen someone stay up as much..." Adaleen added looking tenderly at her brother with a rare sense of compassion that she doesn't normally show to people.

"Well if I could ask one thing it's just that you maybe bath a little more, cuz Jasper, some of the smells I have gotten from you shouldn't exists," Jacob added with a playful smile. Everyone was happy for the first time in a while; chatting away about things. Jacob left the room and returned with a large cut of venison. They hadn't any bread but Lina cooked it into steaks and threw some potatoes on the grate.

"It's good we eat a bit early today, Get a good start on tomorrow. Lina, I don't think wearing the dress to the square is the best idea... do you think we should go and come back for a change just before the fire and dancing," Jacob said as he sat at the table. "We want you presentable to the right people..." he added looking to Adaleen for support.

"I think that's a grand idea, we can hit the vendors and games and come back after midday, to bath and change you into your dress," Adaleen confirmed. "Plus, when the snot nosed kids in town get a look at you after you change into your real gown, oh I would pay to see their faces."

"You kind of did, all worth it though love," Jasper added with a wink.

Lina went back to checking dinner and flipped the steaks over and rolled the potatoes. She riled the fire under the potatoes to get them to cook through while leaving the heat under the steaks alone. She couldn't have pulled the smile from her face if you her wanted to. Not long after that they were all sitting at the table eating. Jasper pulled out bottle of some liquid the others were taking swigs from. They offered it to Lina, but she smelled it and declined.

"By the way Lina, I hope you don't mind but I borrowed those berries you had hanging just there... I'm making a jug of wine with them," Adaleen told her. Lina had almost forgotten about the berries she had been so busy; she had no plan for them and assured Adaleen that it was fine that she had grabbed them.

"Well it will be done in a while we will have it together, maybe at your wedding with the prince... oh." Adaleen cursed at herself for spoiling the surprise.

"The prince... it's going to be the prince, I thought surely it would be some random court member not the actual prince…" Lina's chest got tight, her breathing became erratic as she looked panic-stricken at Adaleen.

"Relax little Lina, it is going to be all right." Adaleen cooed at Lina with a strong smell of the liquid wafting towards her. "Everything is going to be perfect."

That night, after they had eaten, and the twins started singing ballads of the old, they all went gratefully to sleep. Lina lingered awake for a short while after Adaleen had done her usual pass out, thinking about the next day and all the special promises it could bring. She knew she had to be seen, but given her soft yellow hair and stunning hazel eyes she already stood out from the rest of town. She started wondering about her daydreams as they hadn't come of late. The vivid moments where she suddenly feels she is in another place entirely. Just then, the room started to drift away, or rather she did… It was as if she was gently carried into a black sling and then gently dropped on a huge feather bed surrounded by rich silk and heavy but soft blankets. The pillows were squishy, and the room was large and made of brick. The same man she always saw stood at the fireplace stoking the fire patiently.

"Is this real?" Lina questioned aloud confused why now she suddenly fell into a daydream. She sat up and looked around as the man looked to her and his face paled.

"You again, are you real?" he asked her uncertain if she was there. "Or am I going crazy…" He looked away as if she wasn't watching him.

"I'm real but I wasn't here before... who are you?" she asked him imploring into his eyes and pleading with her face.

"Why are you haunting me..." he suddenly yelled throwing a chalice of wine at Lina. Lina threw her arms up to protect herself and felt herself thump down in her own bed. The sound of Adaleen gently snoring arose and she opened her eyes to her regular room. She was so confused, why would she have a daydream like that? She looked at the arms of her sleeping dress and saw red wine stains setting on the fabric.

"So it is real..." she said to herself as she laid back again and closed her eyes finally exhausted. Lina didn't know who the man was but they had seen each other, and he didn't know why either. She drifted off to sleep thinking of the handsome man holding out his hand to her.

The next day Lina woke and considered the events of the past night for a moment. She groggily woke and realized it was the day of the festival and also, she had overslept. When she finally made her way to the kitchen, she saw she was the last to rise, and breakfast was already cooking.

"Really Adaleen how do you ruin sausages... they're all burnt and wonky..." Jasper picked up a scorched sausage and let it thud back to the plate with a crisp sound like it cracked...

"Well if you're so great at cooking why don't you do it then!" Adaleen said raising a knife and throwing it expertly at her brother. It landed sharply in the wall over his left shoulder where he sat, frozen...

"Who says I don't like crispy I love crispy... Just got to get past, hmm, the flavor..." Jasper said with a cough as he picked up the sausage and crunched a piece off.

"Sorry Lina, I wanted to let you sleep, it will be a long day and night for us. Jacob went to try and sell some meat with the cart at the manor. He will be back soon. Oh and I found something growing nearby, I'll show you later, here, try this."

Lina sat at the table as Adaleen poured her some coffee and added the pulp leaf to it. She then feverishly stirred it around and proudly handed the cup to Lina. Lina took the cup curiously and swirled its contents... it was not appealing but seeing the look of hope on Adaleen's face she had to at least try it. She carefully brought the cup to her lips and poured the sweet liquid into her mouth.

"Mmm..." Lina set back the cup and licked her lips. The bitter taste from the coffee was gone.

"Yea this leaf, it only grows about six to eight inches high but it's insides are sweet, and it's safe." Adaleen showed her the slightly thick green leaf and the pulp that could be squeezed out.

"I wouldn't use too much though. Gets me a bit jittered if I use it on more than one drink," Jasper told Lina while still attempting to eat without a look of disgust. Lina picked up a burnt sausage and tried to cut it in half. It cut halfway then gave and broke... she tried her hardest to suppress a giggle as Jasper full-on turned away to cover his mouth.

"All right I'm not the best cook, but at least we have food…" Adaleen said also picking up a burnt sausage with an unsatisfied look on her face. "That won't matter anyway, if Jacob sells even half that cart, your taxes for the quarter will be handled and we will have enough to buy food at the stalls. That reminds me, he should be back pretty soon, Lina you should go pick out your dress and do your first wash up, we will do your hair and a full bath later." Adaleen shooed Lina away from the table. Lina grabbed the cup of sweet coffee and nursed it walking back to the room. She wasn't hungry and there was no room for food in her stomach with that knot of nerves there. Today could be the beginning of the rest of her life. She wondered if she deserved the support, she had heard Adaleen telling Jacob, 'Lina has to have a chance with the royal if you plan to marry her off soon, it is only fair.' She was sure he would be stricken by her at first sight. Jacob didn't sound as sure but agreed to allow her the chance because he didn't think she would ever trust his motives if he didn't. She wanted to be a princess, and he told her all her life she was but he didn't owe her this.

Adaleen came into the room with a pail to fill the wash basin and a cleanish rag. She set them on the ground and left, closing the door behind her. Lina poured the cold water in the basin and set her cleanest normal dress on the bed. It was the blue dress her mother had worn. It was still a little too big on her but with her body changes it was starting to fit slightly better. Catching more at her hips and breast and accentuating her figure. Lina dragged her fingers through her hair with water dampening them to get it all sorted flat from the night before, then dipped the rag and scrubbed gently at her face. She scrubbed her cheeks and chin, her nose and forehead. She felt the spot where she had bumped her head, and noticed it no longer hurt and the bump was all but gone. She scrubbed at her face a bit more than rinsed it with the water. She then did a quick scrub on her arms then legs starting from the top to clean any unnoticed mess. She bled less now, barely any at all, but she still took the cloth and wore it just in case. To finish, she grabbed the waist sheath that she had been gifted and slid the belt around her midsection further accentuating her curves and slightly ruffling the bottom of the dress and tightening the top.

Lina admired the outfit for a moment knowing she would wear a shoulder bag to hide the sheath: she was excited to go out. She felt safer with the knife after having learned how to pull and wield it from Adaleen but she knew she couldn't actually use it if she had to. She hadn't trained with it or anything, but it was a nice accessory to feel safe. She opened the door and walked down the hall to find Jacob had just returned and had a warm, welcoming smile that had to mean good news.

"The Manor didn't have a turkey, and needed bacon venison and rabbit. They paid the above asking because they were so happy someone had extra to sell. Apparently, they were close to offering a reward of twenty gold for a turkey for the evening..." Jacob said throwing a bag of silver and gold coins on the table.

"Sounds like you showed up just a touch to early then bud..." said Jasper with a chuckle clapping Jacob on the back. "Looks like you did all right but we have got to talk about your timing..."

Jacob grabbed Jasper around the waist and threw him over his shoulder...

"Excuse me ladies just one more pig for the spit." Jacob started laughing and ran with Jasper over his shoulder to the door. Jasper dangled helplessly crying about the unfairness of brute strength.

"Will you two get a hold of yourselves... It's time to go to the festival and have some fun!" Adaleen looked at Jacob as if to scold him but couldn't hides her excitement or smile. Jacob put Jasper down and they laughed as he went to the table to divey up the money. He put a decent amount off for the city and broke the rest into three piles. Lina cocked her head to the side wondering why she was getting cut out and noticed one pile was larger than the other two.

"Me and your brother decided I'd stay closest to you through the day and afternoon. So I'll carry the money for us both, that way I can keep an eye on you and... your big brother here can't scare off the prince," Adaleen told Lina grabbing her hand for reassurance. She looked towards Jacob at the end, and he shrugged the statement off.

"You're twice as scary than me to an intelligent person..." He bit back leaning into his chair. He pushed the pile of coins to Adaleen, and she pulled out a bag to stow them on her person. Jasper grabbed his and did the same. Jacob looked at his sister and suddenly a look of concern washed over his face.

"Try to have a good time today. Before you come dress for tonight, allow yourself to enjoy this, try to be a kid one last time…" He gave Lina a weak apologetic smile that warmed her heart.

"All right before you guys start getting too mushy lets go get some actual grub," Jasper said as he casually tossed his barely eaten sausage in the fireplace… "I could eat a prince right now…" Lina fell into a fit of giggles as she rose from the table and moved towards the door with her favorite people in the whole world. Adaleen took point for a moment as they headed towards the street, but then fell back to walk with Lina at her side. The boys trailed behind them, and Jasper was blowing on a makeshift whistle he had made and signing a made-up song about the festival.

Walking towards the festival, they started hearing music play and more and more villagers were heading out of their house towards the square. The sounds of creaking carriages filled with food had become frequent over the last few days but suddenly all that could be heard was joyful conversing, laughter, and music. They were still a few streets away from the square when the first stands popped up. Most of them were food stands. Jasper practically ran up to one with roasted squirrel sticks. The group followed as he paid the man for four sticks of the squirrel. Lina took the squirrel from him and looked at it curiously. She watched as he bit into it and saw his excitement double. The square chunked meat on the stick had a gooey sauce on it but the meat looked seasoned and evenly roasted. Lina smelled the meat and got a smell of sweet maple that made her mouth water. She took a bite and her eyes widened with the flavor profile. She had no idea you could make squirrel taste this good, it was roasted perfectly with a crispy outside and the seasonings not only complimented the meat but the syrup or sauce or whatever it was. She saw her brother and friends tearing the meat quickly off the sticks and was unashamed to mirror them. They had wandered away from the stall and were licking their fingers and moving again towards the festival. They were right next to the square when Jacob grabbed everyone and pulled them to a corner.

"All right, now that we are here, I want to make sure we are all on the same page. Adaleen you and Lina will be leaving at some point, so I think it's best we don't go worrying about seeing and finding you guys until the fire. If, at any point, something happens or goes wrong we meet at home—if that isn't an option we meet at the willow on the river; me and Adaleen already discussed this." Jacob nodded towards Adaleen. Lina knew Jacob and Jasper would probably be together the whole night buying pints and playing cards and games, maybe talking to a few women. She was optimistic that her and Adaleen were about to have the best day of their lives, she wondered for a second why her brother thought something might go wrong, but let the thought pass as a person dressed up on stilts caught her attention over the crowd.

"Can we go now, can we go into the festival?" Lina asked pointing at the man on stilts to Adaleen…

"Yes, you can go…" Jacob said as Adaleen looped an arm through Lina's. She twisted them round and headed towards the opening to the square. The street was thick with travelers and merchants and the stalls and stands littered the sides in every direction, they made their way through the crowd to the square where there was a giant banner going across the opening that read,

'Welcome to the spring Festival'.

Chapter 6

Walking under the banner and into the actual square, Lina couldn't stop twisting and turning to see things. She smelled food's she had never tried and saw booths with strange fruits and berries she had never seen. She saw games with money prizes and pets and animals to be won. She saw a raffle with an animal in a cage labeled, 'Magic creature'. Lina gasped as she saw a webbed blue hand reach out of the bars. She wanted to go towards the cage, but it was against the crowd.

"Anything over there you want to look at we will have to go to later, this way." Adaleen with Lina hooked at her elbow pulled Lina to a bow stand with all kinds of fancy ribbons and hair bows. They also had some hats and veils and gloves displayed behind them. "Fancy something fancy?" Adaleen asked Lina looking at the pretty ribbons. Lina looked about for a moment and then her eyes locked on a ribbon of the same material as her dress, she pointed it out to Adaleen whose eyebrows swept up in surprise.

"Good eye, how much for this." She began to barter with the shopkeeper on the price of the ribbon. Not a moment but a silver coin less they walked away happy with their success.

"We should find you a fancy necklace but let's play some games huh? Could be fun and maybe we will win!" Adaleen steered the way towards a game where you throw a ball into a small vase. The ball was light and bounced easily, no one could land the throws how they wanted. "Not this one, it's rigged," Adaleen said watching the ball 'somehow' evade yet another spot-on throw.

"How about this one," Lina said pulling Adaleen to a dart throwing stand.

"Oooh good eye." Adaleen stepped up and paid for a few throws. She got three bullseyes and won, the gamer asked if she wanted a bigger prize and went again. She then chose her prize. A box of some sweet confection called Carmel. Lina and Adaleen tore off pieces of the sticky sweet confection and popped it in their mouths.

Lina chewed and chewed the delicious sweet. She had never had something so delicious before. It was sticking to her teeth, and she licked the insides and pried it off with her tongue. Adaleen pulled off another piece and offered it which Lina took happily, then she folded the remainder up and put it in her bag.

"We won't be able to explain what this is to the boys, better save some," she said with a wink. They started walking the square and saw that on the far end there were tables and benches set up for people to eat. Lina saw a stall selling corn with butter and asked if they could get some and watch the entertainers by the stand. Adaleen agreed and they both got a treat and went to watch the jugglers and performers. At one point a clown came by startling

Adaleen, she threw a silver coin at him to get him to go away. They sat for a while relaxing as the music kept playing in the background. Lina could see the band in the square playing away looking happy and content, surely making a decent amount in tips.

Lina was looking towards the pub when she thought she saw Jacob. She looked around but couldn't see Jasper anywhere, however Jacob didn't seem to be alone. At first Lina thought the cloaked person must be a girl, but then wondered why they were cloaked and kept watching. Jacob and the stranger had come from the pub and were walking around the side of it. They began talking with the strangers back to Lina . Jacob looked worried and seemed to be arguing with whoever it was. Suddenly the person threw up their hands and walked away leaving Jacob standing alone. He looked as though he was struggling with something but decided it was okay and walked back around the pub to the front and inside.

"Not daydreaming now, are you? Not with all this to keep you entertained." Adaleen poked Lina back to the present moment and pointed at two body contortionists who were impossibly holding each other up.

"No, no, I'm here. Where should we go next?" Lina decided her brother was probably bartering with the stranger and put the encounter out of her mind.

"Well we could always look for a necklace to finish your outfit," Adaleen said pointing towards the jewelry booths back by where the cage had been.

"Okay can we look at the magic creature? I have never seen one before." Lina asked with excitement.

"Yea if it's still there we can…" said Adaleen who didn't look as fond about the idea. "Stay away from it though they can be dangerous," Adaleen warned.

"You have seen them before?" Lina asked with wonder in her eyes.

"In the forest… twice… I would rather not encounter either of those type again, me and Jasper barely escaped the last one. Lost one of our hideouts in the process…" Lina saw a visible shiver go down Adaleen's back as they rose from the benches and locked arms to hear across the square which proved difficult in the dense crowd. They moved slowly towards the outskirts and found the flow of traffic and followed it past more booths filled with all kinds of things. One had perfumes and powders of all different colors and scents, Another they passed contained dried grinded up spices Lina had never seen before. She almost asked to stop when she remembered where they were going and fell back in line with Adaleen refusing to get distracted. She wanted to see that creature.

"Looks like merchandise is getting pretty picked through, look at these first will you." Adaleen had finally reached the jewelry stands. "Don't worry, if it was a raffle, they won't do it till the very end," she added seeing Lina look for the cage frantically. She stopped and looked at the table in front of her covered in jewelry.

"Have you got anything… nicer?" Adaleen asked fingering a fake gold necklace with a sour look on her face.

"Well, we do have a few in back that are a bit pricier…" the woman merchant replied looking doubtful that the two girls could afford anything at all. Adaleen pulled out her money bag and pulled out two gold coins. The weary merchant took one and tried to bend it, then gave it a bite and handed it back.

"All right then come round here…" The large woman ushered them around the table to a another that sat behind her. "These are all fine metals and real semi fine stones… I can't let any go for less than two gold coins…" she added eyeing the pouch of money Adaleen held.

"If any of this looks worthy I'll pay what I have to for it." Adaleen tossed up the two gold coins she had in her hand and caught them both expertly inside the pouch, then gripped it again and stowed it inside her jacket. Lina was looking at the few necklaces they had laid out. Only one looked like it would suit the rest of her outfit. It was a chocker, with a pretty silver pendant in the middle that looked like a bird, and in the middle of the bird was a little purple gem. Lina looked at it a moment and picked it up while the woman eyed her closely.

"This one I think…" she told Adaleen who reached out for the necklace. She weighed it in her hand and looked at the gem inside the pendant.

"How much for this one?" she asked with disinterest. The woman not missing a beat barked her price.

"That'll be six gold pieces…"

"Are you barking? I'll do three and you will be lucky to have gotten that." Adaleen bartered.

"All right, five, that is real silver on not just the pendant but the clasps, and a real fae amethyst stone, even five is a loss on my end…"

Adaleen thought for a moment and looked at Lina, she reached out and lifted her chin looking at her neck…

"All right five it is, but you throw in a pair of silver stud earrings or I'll walk."

Adaleen looked hard at the merchant who considered the offer for a moment before nodding. Adaleen pulled out the bag that contained the hair ribbon and added the chocker and the earrings the merchant handed her before safely tucking them away in her jacket again. Lina reached up and touched her ears and felt the holes that had been pierced in them when she was a small child. She had sold the studs her mother had given her a few winters back to get her mother medicine when they needed it and hadn't worn any since. It was nice to finally be able to think about jewelry and how she was really dressing up as a woman to impress a royal tonight. She looked down, sad for a moment that her parents wouldn't be there to see her dressed up.

"Are you ready to go find your creature?" asked Adaleen making creepy movements with her hands. She smiled at Lina who was sure she had noticed the change in her and smiled back. She was happy to be here, and she owed so much of this to Adaleen, she deserved to have a good day with her.

"Yea, it was over there…" Lina pointed in the direction the cage had been. They linked arms and weaved through the bustling crowd towards the area she had pointed. Once closer they noticed they were not the only townies that had noticed. Marisol, Amanda, and Riana stood near the cage, Amanda was distracting the guard flirting with him while Marisol and Riana held up sticks and poked into the tiny cage, which would rustle every time they did it. They turned and looked at Lina, Marisol pointing her nose even higher in the air, dropped the stick and let out a repugnant giggle.

"Just when I thought this was getting boring... Lina look at you..." Amanda and Riana got in line behind Marisol and walked towards where Adaleen and Lina stood. With Adaleen between them they couldn't do anything to Lina and they knew that but they wouldn't walk away without trying to get on her nerves.

"That's quite enough I think..." Adaleen warned pulling her jacket back and revealing a knife...

"Wouldn't want you going and ruining this beautiful day for us all now would we..." Adaleen stepped forward threateningly. Marisol took a small step back and looked over Adaleen's shoulder to Lina...

"Why waste my time, I have the rest of your life in this village to remind you, that you are exactly where you're supposed to be. Exactly where you belong..." Marisol got cut short by Adaleen taking another step closer and drawing her knife which pulled a little attention from the people around them.

"I said... that's enough..." Adaleen left no joke or hint to be interpreted with her words. They were final and the conversation was over. She stared daggers into Marisol's eyes who faltered immediately. Marisol turned and stalked off with her friends behind her and not another word. Clearly upset at the disrespect of the situation, Adaleen replaced her blade quickly and casually as if nothing had even happened and stepped back to loop her arm with Lina's once more. They stepped forward and saw the small cage propped up on the table for a raffle along with miscellaneous 'magic' items for sale. Lina went by the cage and looked in to the bars, a small grayish-blue animal was sitting inside looking depressed and hurt. Lina felt terrible and instinctively reached her hand out wanting to help the creature. Sensing her presence the small creature looked up at Lina and met her eyes. She looked in its big sad eyes as it reached its little hand up to the bars. Lina reached out and felt someone grab her hand. The merchant had been watching closely.

"I wouldn't miss... small or not it can take your arm off, I have seen it," the man warned jabbing a thumb in the creature's direction.

The cage suddenly filled with a low growl as the little eyes narrowed in the direction of the merchant. Lina pulled her arm away from this man as Adaleen walked forward taking a look herself in the cage.

"That's a baby that is. What is it anyway?" she asked looking at the merchant directly.

"Some sort of water creature... finds water and some other stuff or something..." the merchant said dismissively as if he couldn't care less. Lina felt rage, rage she had never known at the man. He was letting them hurt this poor creature, it's just a little baby and he treats it like its nothing. She looked at Adaleen and said she wanted a ticket; she wanted the animal.

"Uh… can we talk about that a minute…" Adaleen pulled Lina to the side and looked at her with as much compassion as she could. "These raffles are rigged… the big-ticket items like that always end up back with the merchant to pretend to sell at the next meeting… plus I have enough to feed us tonight, but that necklace was expensive…" The reality that Lina couldn't do anything to get that animal out of that cage made her heart plummet… She was devastated…

"Adaleen I can't, I have to help…" Lina pleaded with Adaleen with her eyes beginning to tear up. She had been the daughter and sister of a hunter her whole life. She knew what kind of animals belonged in cages and when she looked in those eyes, she knew that was not one of them. Adaleen grabbed Lina's hands… and held her eyes.

"I didn't like it either they usually don't use such young creatures but what can we do about it…" She released Lina's hands and tied her fingers together swinging her arms behind her head in thought. A passersby hit her elbow and complained loudly about people being rude and then she stopped…

"Let's go see what Jasper thinks… we have a bit of time before you have to be ready… and I know what pub he likes." Adaleen had a warm smile on her face, and Lina couldn't tell if this was a mission or a distraction, but seeing no other way she followed Adaleen again through the crowd towards the pub the had went to running from Berry. When they got inside, there was barely an empty table, but they heard Jasper right off. He was near the middle of the room winning a game of cards. Adaleen and Lina walked up as the table began to clear out. A barmaid walked up and started picking up the empty cups, glasses and mugs.

"Thank you, another mead, please…" Jasper who is sweeping his winnings into a pile tipped the waitress a silver coin as Adaleen and Lina sat down.

"Jacob part ways with you for drinking the whole pub, or cheating on cards?" Adaleen asked watching her brother hiccup and stash the coins in a purse.

"Cheat, you know what crowds like this will do to a cheater? Nah. He went to grab us some minced pies should be back any minute. Why?"

"Lina why don't you go to the bar and order us a drink each?" Adaleen handed Lina a silver coin and Lina slid off the bench to go get them drinks still looking a little sad. When she got up to the bar, she asked the barmaid for two ciders and paid with the silver coin. The lady put two mugs in front of her and Lina carried them back to the table and saw Jasper and Adaleen with their heads together. Lina knew them well enough to know when they were up to something, but they pulled apart before she sat back down.

"I hope you have been having fun today, Lina. All things considered." Jasper looked curiously over at Lina who tried her best to smile and get the image of the big sad eyes out of her head. She picked up her cider and took a sip to pull away from Jasper's gaze.

"Shall we eat her or grab a quick on the way back to yours? We have to get you bathing soon!" said Adaleen who clearly planned to stay on task.

"On the way, I want to try something else new," Lina answered after thinking a moment.

"Oh shoot I almost forgot." Adaleen dug into her bag a moment and pulled out the big gob of Carmel wrapped in paper. "You have to try this," she said handing it to Jasper who looked it over with a look of repulsion at first. He poked it a few times, then smelled it. He finally tore some off and stuck it in his mouth and suddenly started chewing profusely.

"Well, that is delicious..." Jasper said licking his fingers and going back for more, but Adaleen quickly grabbed it before he could.

"Not too much I'm saving it..." she said and stowed it away in her bag again. She picked up her cider and took a big swig from it. Then checked to make sure Lina was still drinking hers. Lina took a big drink of hers and felt better as the cider filled her belly. Just then, the doors opened and in came Jacob carrying about four minced meat pies. He walked towards the table and saw the girls sitting there and smiled warmly taking a seat beside Lina.

"Didn't think I'd see you so early," he teased Lina and offered her a pie. She declined and took another sip from her cider.

"We are leaving soon to go get her ready, got a couple last-minute things while we were here." Adaleen mentioned the necklace and the hair ribbon while she swept a hand through Lina's hair pulling it off her nick for a moment. It felt nice, sipping the cold cider and having her hair off her even just for a moment. She smiled as she drank the last of her cider. Adaleen drained her cup in probably three swallows and she stood up and stretched. Lina rose too and told Jacob she would see him later and bid Jasper a farewell. They linked arms yet again and headed towards the door.

Lina left the pub feeling much more cheery than when she had arrived, cider had that effect on people. They weaved their way back towards where they entered the square and stopped at one small stand that was selling the smallest fowls on a pike and Lina had to try it. They paid two silver coins and each got a little bird to nibble on the way home. They walked slowly, joking and laughing recounting the different performers and the stands that filled with weird things they had never seen before. Adaleen was using a finger to hold her nose up and pretending to be Amanda, trying to flirt with the merchant. Lina fell into a fit of giggles for a moment, then stopped.

"What's wrong? I thought we hated Amanda and them…" Adaleen asked seeing the change in Lina.

"I do, I'm just… if tonight goes the way you hope… what if I don't get to see you or spend time with you like this again, what if I can't find Jacob and he wants me to go to the palace or something and I can't say goodbye, or… what if he doesn't like me at all…"

Lina suddenly felt the pressure of the situation on her. If it worked her, whole life and the people she loved, all of that would change, and what if it didn't… She couldn't even think about what could happen if he wasn't interested. Adaleen stopped walking and faced Lina.

"Stop worrying about things before they come to pass. It isn't going to do you or me any good. Whatever happens tonight we will work from there. And a true gentleman would never ask you to leave with him without asking to meet your family… so don't call it quits over nothing." Adaleen lifts Lina's face to hers. "We got this." She sounded firm and sure as she sometimes did. They turned and started walking the last bit of way home, Adaleen turned and chucked her bird carcass on the side of the road. Lina held onto hers as she hadn't quite finished it.

They walked the final streets long past midday going back to the cabin and entered feeling tired from the morning's festivities. Lina tended the fire as Adaleen went to fetch water from the well. They didn't have time to walk all the way to the river so they agreed to just use four pails of well water to clean her. When Adaleen got back, she poured the water in the basin and told Adaleen to strip down. She then helped her scrub her body using the water and soaked her hair. Lina felt a little raw from the scrubbing but didn't complain.

Adaleen started combing her fingers through Lina's hair trying to layer out pieces as best she could to braid it. Lina began to ask her to leave a piece down to hide the bump on her head but when she reached up to feel it, it was gone.

"Must have cleared up, luckily, just in time." Adaleen crooned as she began to put all of Lina's hair into a braid the middle of her hair. The braid came down her head to the side and into a ponytail. Adaleen had worked the ribbon into the braid somehow, Lina's wasn't sure where she learned to do this but knew Adaleen braided her own hair often. Nothing quite as delicate or complicated as this, but simple braids. When Adaleen finished, she tied the end of the ribbon around the bottom of her hair securely. Then she lifted the dress out of the box. The beautiful, soft purple on the top was a perfect color for spring, and as the dress' hip skirt went down it turned to a darker bolder purple with a beautiful silver lining. The discreet yellow flowers on the dress pattern matched Lina's hair perfectly. Adaleen looked at Lina and smiled as she handed her the pale-yellow short heels that she had found for her. Lina put on the shoes and turned for Adaleen to put on her necklace. She stood still while she attached the chocker, and put in her silver earrings. Lina reached up and touched the braid as Adaleen went to the vegetable stash and pulled out a little jar Lina hadn't noticed over there. Adaleen opened the jar and told Adaleen to close her eyes and pout out her lips. Adaleen applied the fruit pulp carefully to her lips and cheekbones to then rubbed her cheekbones for a bit. She stood back and looked at Lina and smiled.

"Now you look like a queen..." she said and hugged her. " Oh also." She took Lina's hand and ran it threw the fabric on the side of the dress revealing a hidden pocket containing a sheath. "This is the surprise; your knife I gave you should fit snug and hidden. Surprise," Adaleen added with a smile.

"I thought the shoes were the surprise." Lina looked down at the nice shoes that were on her feet they were a little big, but she preferred that to the tight old shoes. Adaleen went to her room to get Lina's knife from the sheath and Lina went to the vegetables and pulled some greens and potato out to cut up. She quickly tore a chicken wing from the carcass and put it and the greens in a rag and tied it up. She then put the rag in her bag as Adaleen returned to the room. She handed Lina the knife which she secured in the sheath. Sure enough, it was completely hidden from sight.

"Now we are ready." Adaleen stepped towards the door and opened it as Lina put her bag on her shoulder and followed. "You can't carry that... here I got it." And Adaleen whisked the bag away from Lina. She followed her out into the darkening sky.

"They should be lighting the bonfire soon if they haven't. Just enough time to hopefully make an entrance." Adaleen mused as they marched towards the square. Lina suddenly felt nervous. She had never worn such nice things and was sure she looked great but other women would surely dress up tonight too. She could barely afford to do any of this, and couldn't even imagine it without the twins' help. She didn't want to let them down, so she walked lightly not dragging her feet watching her shadow holding her head up high.

As they moved towards the square, the sun dipped lower and lower out of sight, and the sounds of the festival dying down reached them as older participants went home merchants cleaned their stalls up and the rest went to the bonfire behind Crestfallen Manor. They came to the banner they crossed beneath twice before and found the square clearing as torches were lit lining the way to the bonfire and illuminating the stragglers. Lina looked over and saw the cage and reached for her bag on Adaleen.

"What are you…" Adaleen questioned as Lina reached in the bag and pulled out the rag with food.

"Distract the merchant while I sneak him food." Lina slowly worked her way around the booth next to the cage as Adaleen walked up to flirt with the merchant and ask about the raffle. Lina worked her way to the cage and locked eyes with the animal again. With the man totally distracted she shoved the greasy little satchel into the cage through the bars. The animal looked down and sniffed it then wiggled it open with his teeth and started eating the potatoes greens and fowl. It looked at Lina for a moment before it continued to eat the food. Lina moved away from the cage and to Adaleen's side. She then noticed a cloaked figure standing nearby, she was sure they had seen her but they weren't saying anything. Adaleen bid goodnight to the man, and they turned to head towards Crestfallen Manor. Lina looked back one last time at the little cage and it's occupant, and hoped he would get sold to someone good.

Chapter 7

Adaleen led Lina along the torches to the walkway to Crestfallen Manor where the last few people were making their way to the back. As they began to pass the side of the manor, they began to hear the music and laughter. The manor rose to a cliff and the cliff overlooked the field. Once here the festival attendees took the slope down the hill to the huge bonfire. The manor had a large stone overlooking the ones they used to address crowds. A man stood there waiting for attention. The man was the well-dressed Lord Renfeild of Crestfallen Manor. The crowd began to quiet as he held up his hand. Adaleen and Lina stopped on the hill to listen with a few others.

"This has been one of the finest spring festivals Crestfallen village has *ever seen*..." he begins to a cheer erupting through the crowd as people yelled out in agreement. "The food has been delicious. The games enthralling and the entertainment was gallant." He motioned to a crew of jesters, who, on cue, juggled batons set ablaze and blew fire towards the crowd. who applauded and hooted before quieting down again. "If this festival has anything to say about the coming year..."

Lina had stopped looking at the lord or listening to what he said. She was suddenly staring right at the man just behind him. He had sandy reddish-brown hair and a royal crest on his suit. And his cool blue eyes were staring at Lina. They held each other's gaze for a moment, While Lina blocked out all the other things going on and then the man was pulled forward. He had just missed his introduction...

"And here to bestow his grace and honor upon us is Prince Dalton of Aliyen Kingdom itself." The whole crowd erupted with applause as the prince looked out and waved, he again turned towards the hill and Lina and Adaleen and looked right at Lina.

"Hello, Hello all of you thank you so much, I have come on behalf of my family to show Crestfallen village our thanks for your support, we as a kingdom have never been stronger..."

The prince was cut off by a loud explosive noise coming from the front of the building. Suddenly, Lina looked up and saw smoke was rising up on the other side of the manor in the distance. Barely visible in the night sky, she saw what looked to be fires, and lots of them. There was a scream far off in the distance, as people slowly began to panic. The prince was swept back by the royal guard and Lina looked out to him as he looked back where she stood before Adaleen whipped Lina around and started back up the hill. They hadn't totally entered so they were close to the exit. People were now appearing at the other side of the field. Lina didn't know what was happening but the screams and panic were intensifying.

"Adaleen..." she started to say.

"Later Lina, let's get someplace safe first." They tore up the last of the hill, started jogging around the manor and began to run through the square with the buildings and market not yet burning. Lina looked back and saw something had happened to the manor, that's what the sound was. Off to the left she heard people screaming and saw the fires building to the tops of the homes and businesses. They ran through the square that was still somewhat empty past where the merchant had been with his crate. Nowhere to be seen, they continued on at a quick run keeping ahead of anyone else who came out.

"But Adaleen, Jacob what about Jacob..." Lina was starting to hurt from the shoes and stumbled for a minute. Adaleen stopped and took them off her feet.

"We have a plan remember meet at the house, if not there, the willow," Adaleen told her, grabbing her hand and pushing farther yet still. They stumbled down the street as the smoke began to rise. Lina saw that people's cabins were ablaze.

They worked their way running through the streets towards the back corner of town. They made it to the street next to Lina's and saw some men in dark leathers running with torches. The girls hid until they left only to see five more after them come from behind some cabins further down the streets. Lina was very aware of the sounds of screaming and cries for help she heard distantly.

"We are gunna have to make a run for it, and hope your cabin is still up." Adaleen grabbed hold of Lina's hand and they stood together. The smoke gave them some cover as they ran across the street and through a yard to reach her home. They arrived at the front and saw the cabin burning. They walked around to the back and that was where they saw Jasper, carrying a cage over his head as a man held a sword to his back.

"I said what are you doing here?" the man said with a thick slur to his words.

"I told you I live round here," said Jasper as coolly as Lina had ever heard him sound towards a person. Adaleen grabbed Lina's arm and had her drop down in the bushes. Then Adaleen creeped up very slowly behind the guy holding up her brother. The moment he thought he heard something it was too late she had a knife to his throat and a hand around his mouth before he could even react to dying. The blood only spurt for a moment before streaming down, he fell with a thud and Jasper turned around with the crate still over his head.

"Sister, you have got to teach Jacob a thing or two about timing," he said relaxing slightly. Suddenly another explosive noise shook through the village.

"Where is Jacob?" Adaleen demanded searching her brother's face for answers.

"He was in the field, I told him to go ahead while I did some things that he wouldn't be fond of. I thought I'd have to knock out that merchant for a few then the explosion drove him right off, left this little guy behind to fend for himself so I scooped him up. I was just coming to try and, you know, get the cage open." Jasper looked over at Lina... as she emerged from the bushes and moved closer.

"I don't like babies in cages I don't care the circumstance..." he declared to try and vindicate his action. "Plus I think it likes you." Jasper had put the cage down to his belly and a little blue-gray hand reached towards Lina.

"Well we don't have time we have to get to the willow and wait for Jacob. Find something you can take with you if you must but hurry," Adaleen barked the order clearly feeling impatient as Lina moved out from the bush and went up to the crate. Jasper sat it down and ran into the smoke hut. He came out with a mallet, a bag and a gourd, with smoke trailing off him.

"All right let's get this open. He hit the lock on the cage a few times until it broke open. He opened the door to the cage and the little animal rolled itself out. It stood up on his hind legs with his webbed feet and hands and looked at Lina. She swore she felt it smile.

"I'm sure that's better, but we have to go now..." She gestured to her cabin which was burning behind her. The baby creature reached his hands up to be picked up and Lina did so, hugging him close to her.

"All right now let's go before someone else..." As the words were leaving Adaleen's mouth more rebels showed up around the neighbors, they turned to look in the direction of the dirty little cabin where it almost sounded like there was talking but, the entire group had already gone in the forest.

Hunched down in the weeds walking with the trees, Lina followed Adaleen while holding the baby animal close to her with Jasper following behind. They stayed in the tree line to remain hidden and didn't see any people. Lina wished they would get to the tree they would be able to look at the smoke from there at least. She tried to remember anyone behind her, but she only remembered a few people making it out from the field for sure.

"Can we stop a minute?" Lina asked Adaleen. Adaleen looked around and nodded then moved them slightly away from the road they had been following. They sat on a stump and caught their breath.

"Someone needs to tell me what in the hell happened..." Jasper said just above a whisper.

"I will as soon as you tell me about the blast, we didn't see that bit at all." Adaleen looked at her brother waiting.

"It's like I said, I decided to steal this." He gestured at the baby animal. "And waited for an opportunity. There was a loud booming sound and a whole bunch of fire and smoke started coming from the manor and pieces of it started falling in." Jasper rubbed the back of his head while he talked. "Then the merchant went to go check on the fire or run away from it, so I grabbed this little guy and got out of there," Jasper finished with shrug.

"Don't think I haven't thought about the fact you left us behind knowing we were headed in... regardless, you said it was fire? Was there colors or powder or magic?"

Adaleen asked with a meaningful look. "Did you see any rebels start something?"

"Not that I saw, I have never seen a fire like that, it just blew its way up out of the building." Jasper answered. "What happened on your end?"

"We were starting down the hill when we were being addressed. Everyone was down in the field when we heard it. I looked beyond the building and there were pillars of smoke climbing to the sky... anyone at the fire would have a hard time seeing the town burning because of the bonfire and the cliff... We turned to run, and got back up the hill, but I saw the rebellion enclosing the people in the field... it didn't look good. I didn't stop to see what was going to happen so I kept running. By the time we made it out of the square, the smoke from the fires were taking our vision... and our breath. They had been slowly burning the town down, they must have started just at dark when everyone was in the field. We only saw a handful of men but I'm sure there were more lurking in the smoke..." Jasper and Adaleen looked at each other. He nodded and said they should get moving, the closer they are to the tree the better, plus he was thirsty.

"Bet you regret drinking so much now huh..." Adaleen whispered back to Jasper, who mocked her subtly.

As the river became visible the baby in Lina's arms started to squirm a bit. They moved down the bank to the willow tree. This is the secluded place Lina goes to do laundry. There are stones to sit and beat clothes on and it's hidden from the road by the tree and the dip down. The baby wiggled and wiggled as she set him down on his legs.

Lina looked at the baby animal taking in its appearance. It was gray-blue all over with hints of green. It had tiny scales all over its body and a slight exterior spine. His mouth was almost bill-shaped but she knew he had teeth of some sort. She touched a little webbed hand, and he grasped it lightly. Then she noticed he had little fins on his face that reared up when he was happy... He looked at her and rubbed his eyes, then ran to the water's edge and jumped in, then rose to the water's surface and allowed his head and eyes to sit out from the water. Lina smiled at him as he disappeared beneath the surface.

"Will it come back you think?" Jasper asked looking at the water, suddenly his answer came as the animal came out of the water on all fours went up to Lina and dropped a dead fish at her feet then ran back to the water. The fish was pretty small, but she still smiled at it and picked it up surprised by the baby's speed.

"What are you going to name it?" Adaleen asked Lina sitting on a rock and looking towards her.

"I don't know. What about Frills?" She said aloud to the twins.

"Frills the sea creature. that's great actually. All right Frills chills..." Jasper said cementing the name on the spot. Frills swam around in the river watching everyone at the shore and every now and then diving for a fish.

"So Lina had the prince's eye before the explosion..." Adaleen casually mentioned. Lina began to blush a deep red, she hadn't realized Adaleen had seen that moment.

"Really? Too bad things had to end before they got started ay..." Jasper smiled approvingly.

"I hate to ask but... we are going to need clothes and supplies Jasper." Adaleen looked at her brother. He nodded.

"I figured I should run to the closest hideout and see what we got stored. It isn't too far from here," Jasper started. He looked down at Lina and told her he would keep his ears open for people and word of Jacob. And then Jasper slipped off as silent as a cat in the night. Frills popped his head up and Lina saw the moon shine in his eyes and flash away when he blinked.

"You should lay down for a bit. I'm going to keep watch because we can't start a fire. We wouldn't want to draw attention to ourselves right now. We will wait for Jacob until tomorrow." Adaleen took off her jacket and draped it on Lina who accepted it gratefully after suddenly noticing the cool breeze coming off the river. Lina looked up above the trees and saw a huge billowing cloud of smoke rising to the sky. Everything was gone, they burned and broke it all, her whole life was about to change. Lina thought about her home one last time before she drifted off to sleep.

Lina slept through the night and awoke bright and early to the twins bickering amongst themselves as usual.

she slightly moved and noticed Frills laying up under her arm softly snoring.

"Neeeeem mamamamama… neeeem mamamamama… neeeeem mamamamama"

Lina giggled at the funny noise and the movement caused Frills to wake up with a sneeze. He blinked his big eyes and shook his head and looked up to Lina with what she was sure was a smile.

"Oh thank God, please, Lina… she is trying to cook again." Jasper had just noticed Lina had opened her eyes. Lina got up and stretched and rubbed her eyes. She looked over at the twins and saw a small fire and a poorly made spit to cook food along with a bag of meats, dried and salted and a couple raw. Lina got up and walked over and pulled out the raw sausages and put them evenly spaced on the spit then placed them high over the fire.

"I will be right back" Lina said as she went to go relieve herself in the woods. She scurried out of sight and struggled with lifting the nice dress and not having shoes. After Lina had gone, she came back to the fire and gave the sausages a quarter turn. Adaleen was lounging in a tree overlooking the willow.

"Jacob never showed up?" Lina asked already knowing the answer to her question.

"No he hasn't yet. But don't worry we won't give up on him," Jasper told Lina. Frills scurried along the rocks and found a warm one to lay on.

"What if they… took him… or got him… or—" Lina was cut off by Adaleen jumping down from her perch.

"Jacob is a big guy, he isn't easy to 'take', as for the rest, there were over fifteen kings' guards in that building and you may not have noticed but plenty of other guards throughout the crowd. I know last night I said it didn't look good, but realistically, I only saw about fifteen people trying to close in so unless they waited to use their major firepower, I doubt the town was taken or anything like that," Adaleen answered looking Lina in the eye. Lina noted Adaleen looked very tired and realized she had probably not slept.

"Here... You need different clothes..." Adaleen thrusted some of her own dark pants and a shirt and jacket at Lina as she again turns the sausages. "I can take out the braid..."

"Leave it for now please... it's less in the way." She took the clothes. She walked off to the woods and quickly got changed. She took off the dress and left her necklace and hair and pulled on the pants shirt and jacket and was tucking the shirt in walking out barefoot looking at Adaleen.

"I had an old pair of boots Jasper brought as well. "Jasper, what are you doing?" Adaleen asked Jasper, exasperated.

"Well I'm digging a hole to put this jug of wine you made in." As Lina came out from the trees, she in fact saw Jasper digging a hole.

"What would you do that for? We could use that jug to carry water..." Adaleen reached towards the jug and Jasper grabbed it and held it fast to his chest...

"But… but then we would have no wine…" Jasper sputtered at his sister.

"We aren't staying here anyway why bury it?" she asked her brother looking defeated.

"Well we might come back for it someday, you never know." Jasper dug and dug he made an impressively large hole then nestled the jug of wine deep in the earth and covered it with at least two-feet of dirt. Once finished he put a dug a rock into the dirt symbolizing the spot.

"What do we do if Jacob doesn't show up?" Lina asked while removing the sausages from the fire. She felt like she knew the answer, but she really wanted to be wrong…

"Well, after this morning, if we don't see him, that means for whatever reason he can't get here. He told me if that were to happen, we were to meet at the waterfall." She looked at Jasper for a moment and sighed. "Weird how he had plans I'd swear if I didn't know him that he knew something," Adaleen said almost thinking aloud.

"I thought it was weird when he mentioned it before yea." Lina recalled thinking it was strange to receive such a dark message in such a bright moment.

"Ya know, he was runnin' around a lot when we got there, I saw him talkin' to a girl in a hood, so I figured she was keep'n him busy." Jasper shrugged as if he hadn't considered any of this alarming.

He took the first sausage and commended Lina's cooking followed by Adaleen who looked as though she might fall over. Lina took a sausage and threw half of it to

Frills who jumped off his rock happily to retrieve the snack. Lina nibbled on her sausage as Jasper told Adaleen she needed to get some sleep. Adaleen attempted to argue until she accidentally hit herself in the face with her sausage because of moving her hands too wildly.

"All right maybe a tiny nap after I eat," Adaleen agreed wiping the grease from her forehead and giggling with Lina. After she finished her sausage, Adaleen curled up next to the spot Lina had slept in. Jasper climbed the tree she had previously been posted in to keep lookout, and Lina went to the edge of the water to play with Frills. He would jump in and pop his head out and blow a stream of water near her then disappear just to jump out and run by her on all fours and back into the water. She tried to catch him and tried to splash him with water which he would expertly dodge. He was slick when he was wet and quick on his feet and in the water. Lina wondered how anyone had been able to catch him at all. She removed her boots and stuck her toes in the water and rolled up the pants. She had put her knife on her side, but her sheath was lost at home. Jasper suddenly threw one down at her from the tree.

"Got an extra couple, thought I should grab one just in case when I grabbed supplies," he said leaning back on the thick branch he was sitting on to get comfortable. Lina strapped the waist sheath through the pants loops and popped her knife in. It wasn't perfect but it would hold, which was all she needed. Frills came out of the water and went and climbed on the rocks as Lina laid back to relax.

Lina woke just passed midday, she hadn't meant to fall asleep and apparently Adaleen had been unceremoniously woken up.

"Ay what the—" She was cut off by Jasper's finger which he pushed to his sister's lips, pointing in the distance towards the road.

"Shut the fire." Adaleen hopped up and ran to where their little fire had basically gone out. she started kicking dirt over it to snuff out the last bit and stop it from smoking while Jasper helped. Lina went and pet Frills down his back as he also slept on a warm rock making his cute little snoring sound. He awoke to her touch and yawned as she reached for him and scooped him up. Lina stooped down and grabbed the spare bag by the water then stepped back into the trees. Once in the trees, they all sat in the bush where they could see the spot they had been and waited.

"Were they coming our way?" Adaleen asked her brother.

"Looked like it," Jasper replied still watching. "All this waiting around has got me on edge though..." Jasper admitted to his sister with a shrug.

"Technically if he hasn't made it here by midday..." Adaleen mentioned pointing up at the sun as reference. "Then he didn't make it time, which means for some reason he can't get here."

Lina grabbed a couple mushrooms that she noticed on the log next to them...

"We can't just leave..." Lina said looking slightly shocked at the suggestion.

"What if he got cut off and already headed that way?" Jasper questioned both girls quietly.

"They would be here by now Jasper," Adaleen said no longer hiding her voice.

"Hey who is out there." Suddenly a large looking man popped up in the clearing. He had a thick woolen shirt the color of mud and a pair of raggedy slacks held up by a rope belt.

"I don't' think there is anyone here any more boss, they probably left this morning," a smaller pale man with a long sharp nose spoke to the first man also popping into the clearing.

"Well good, the longer we don't run into anyone the less trouble we will have," said the first man.

"Keep up you" The man gave a tug on his rope belt with an abnormal amount of length and dragged what looked to be Prince Dalton into view. He was tied up, slightly bruised bleeding and gagged but he was clearly trying to get free.

"Stop that!" The bigger man hit Prince Dalton hard sending him to the ground. Lina looked on in horror and turned to Adaleen. She and Jasper were having a silent conversation with their eyes using random hand gestures along with shakes and nods of the head. When they seemed to have agreed on what they wanted to do they both drew a knife each, Jasper brandishing a second and began to silently move towards the clearing.

"Get me some water you useless mutt…" The bigger man yelled at his smaller friend. The prince still lay motionless out cold from the hit.

"Once he wakes, we will head on towards Took, pass all the way through Branson and see what the royal family is willing to pay for their prized heir." He threw his head back with a throaty laugh that turned into a phlegmy cough. He coughed until his throat cleared and he started to laugh again. It was at that moment he found one of Jaspers blades at his throat. Unable to draw his sword he swung out backwards, catching Jasper off guard. Jasper slashed at his hand when he went for his blade and was almost blindsided by the man's partner. Just in time to be of service Adaleen leapt from above in the tree and landed on the second accomplice forcing him to smash his head on the ground. The first guy was the problem though. He was looking at Adaleen and Jasper like they were toys, he stood over them both and laughed.

"You think you are enough to defeat me?" Just then he felt a thump on his back, the prince was awake and, on his feet, ramming the man with everything he had. He went to reach for his blade again and Adaleen cut his arm this time, deep. He howled out and grabbed his arm as Jasper went for the kill seeing an immediate opening. Jasper thrusted out his knife and connected with the man's throat. The man fell to his knees as blood began to pour down the man's neck, he fell forward on his face and it began to pool around him. Adaleen cut the rope and untied the prince without saying anything. She and Jasper eyed him for a moment.

"Is that..." Jasper asked his sister...

"Sure is..." Adaleen answered.

"I'm sorry but are you two siblings, that was some good co-op fighting and you look fairly similar..." The prince looked to them from one face to the other trying to decipher if they saved him for noble reasons or not.

"Hmmm. *Lina!*" Adaleen yelled out; Lina had been watching from the distance. She slowly made her way back to their spot where she stepped slowly out of the trees with Frills in her arms.

The prince looked at her then did a double take. "Oh no..." He started to nervously look around.

"You were the last thing I saw before the... well everything... you had nothing to do with it right?" The prince looked at Lina and implored her to tell him the truth.

"To do with it, she was only there to see you..." Adaleen answered looking offended. "And now you mention it, funny way to thank someone from savin' them from whatever that just was..." She folded her arms over her chest as Jasper slapped the second man on the ground trying to wake him up.

"Hey Frills... can you?" Jasper filled his cheeks with air and pushed them releasing the air in the direction of the man. Frills jumped down from Lina and ran to the water and filled his mouth and got all the way up to the man and spit the tiniest little stream in his face. He stirred slightly then sat up alert. He touched the back of his head before noticing the people looking down at him, He seemed fine till he noticed Frills right by him on all fours letting out the tiniest little growl... Then he jumped a bit.

"Boss?" he said before noticing his boss' body lying nearby. He turned slightly pale then a little green and got up and tried to run. Jasper tackled him to the ground, and they fought a bit. Finally, Adaleen took the rope and tied him up to get their answers.

"What were you doing holding the prince prisoner like that..." Adaleen asked getting straight to the point.

"Just ransom... it was just for money... I wouldn't a taken him if Rufus hadn't said we should. He was just lying there passed out, no guards or nothing. Please let me go..." He was crying and struggling against the ropes. The story made sense enough that they felt no need to keep him but Adaleen didn't think they should let him go until they were ready to go also.

"We can't have him telling anyone where we are especially if there is a prince around, or this is just the first ransom he deals with..." Jasper told the group. Lina looked at the prince who had been staring at her. He looked away suddenly and color rose to his cheeks like he was embarrassed.

"We can't leave yet we have to wait for Jacob," Lina proclaimed to Jasper.

"Lina we won't have a choice soon, we can't stay here and your cabin is gone," Adaleen gently reminded Lina that the only way through would have to be forward and assured her they would find Jacob. The prince remained quiet a moment then inquired.

"Where is it you plan to go to meet him?" He looked to Adaleen and Jasper the clear leaders of the group.

"The waterfall..." Jasper said quickly catching himself a hit from Adaleen. "Hey what..."

"Well I happen to be going the same way maybe we can travel together?" The prince said hopefully. Adaleen sighed and looked at Lina. She and Jasper put their heads together and whispered a moment.

"What's in it for us?" Adaleen demanded eyes glowering into the prince's.

"I'm sure my father will grant you anything you would like as I am next to be king," replied the prince rolling his hand through the air and smiling.

"If we say yes... you have to change clothes, and no more of this royal prince talk, safer to keep it secret," Adaleen told him in a pushy tone.

"And we are not your servants... you sleep where we sleep eat what we eat and bury your own scat..." added Jasper. "And you will have your share of watches at night you will be expected to stay awake for."

"If we ever start to trust you," Adaleen added.

"All right you guys, I think he gets it, they wouldn't have said no... they just don't want to be pushed around..." Lina moved forward to hand the prince a mushroom. "Are you hungry..."

"Starved..." The prince took the mushroom and put it whole in his mouth not breaking his eyes from Lina's.

"And no more of that..." said Jasper sliding in between the two and putting his arms up in a cross. "She is not just some toy for you 'Milord'." He hung a smugness on the last word. "I mean it, hands to yourself or I'll have two more hands to me self, get me..." Jasper gave the prince a menacing look which he shrugged off...

"All right any more rules? And what am I to wear if not the clothing with my family crest." He looked down at his rather telling attire, understanding how he got spotted to begin with.

"I brought an extra set of clothes, you're about my height and weight should fit enough." Jasper threw a bag at the prince who took it in the woods to change. The rest of the group began to gather their things and discuss how they planned to get to the waterfall.

"I say we cut back to the road and follow it..." Adaleen said to Lina and Jasper.

"It's not safe on the road right now... even with the forest line for cover," Jasper stated.

"Well then what are we going to do..." Adaleen looked at her brother, lost.

"Ahem." Lina cleared her throat getting the twins attention. "We could follow the river..."

Lina remembered The river going straight to the waterfall. Her brother always told her it was the easiest way to get to the kingdom, just go against the current and you end up there.

"That's right, people don't usually go that way because of the woods, but I guess we don't have to worry about that much." Adaleen looked at the prince coming back out of the woods.

"With four of us and our little beasty we should be hard pressed to sneak up on," Jasper commented.

"And with my jewelry we can sell and buy as we need on the way." The prince opened his hand to show it was full of rings and cufflinks he had been wearing.

"Soo it's decided, we go find Jacob at the waterfall. Let's pack up." Lina eagerly started collecting the bags and humming slightly as Frills jumped up into Lina's arms and the prince looked at him with curiosity.

"I'm sorry where did you get him…" the prince asked clearly surprised by the connection between the two.

"Stole him from the fare, why? Gunna turn me in?" Jasper asked given Lina a wink.

"Well no I have just only seen adults before and they are much more aggressive…" he said poking a finger at Frills and yanking it back when frills snapped his jaw at him.

"Well he is with us now… it's a fortnight walk at least." Lina looked at the site to make sure they had not forgotten anything, as she and her friends started what looked to be the makings of a long journey.

Chapter 8

Lina and her group walked on slowly for a few hours, the sun started to dip slightly in the sky.

Jasper had been looking for a small clearing to set up camp and as the day was wearing on, he finally chose a spot.

"We need to keep moving..." Adaleen started to push as he sat down and opened his bag to pull out some salted meats.

"Everyone is tired, I know I'm hungry and we have to make a log of what all we have... We only have so much food, so we need to decide when to start hunting, and we need to discuss where we are willing to stop and trade for money... plus aren't you the least bit curious about how the prince became unconscious and alone..." Jasper finished, looking towards the prince who had sat down and was removing his boots. Frills who had been half walking half galloping beside Lina ran towards the water and did a dive-in head first.

"All right fine we will set up a camp and talk over what he saw after we left... But tomorrow we cover more ground so rest your feet well, you three." She pointed at each of them separately. "What have you got left for cooking?" She looked at Jasper who had three of the six bags carried. He started removing the bags and looking in them... he pulled out a rabbit carcass and a bird.

"The rest is salted or smoked in this bag..." He jabbed his foot at another bag. "You can go with me to get wood together for a fire..." He poked the prince with his elbow who began putting his boots back on and rose to help as told.

"Here." Jasper reached in the bag of salted meats and pulled out four semi-large pieces of jerky and handed it out... "For energy," he said as he took a bite off his. The prince took a very large hungry bite, as they trekked into the woods to find fire wood. Lina took the bag and gourd she had been carrying and set them down. She took the gourd to the river to fill it and Frills came jumping out of the water with a much larger fish than the last time. He sat it on the ground near Lina and ran back to the water.

"Well, at least he is useful..." Adaleen said and scooted the fish further up the bank away from the water.

"Why did Jasper free him?" Lina asked Adaleen realizing now that she never questioned her...

Adaleen got a dark look on her features, and turned away from Lina.

"I think that is a story for another night, to be honest. I'd have to talk with Jasper about it see, it's personal..." Adaleen answered Lina, not meeting her eyes. Lina, having filled the gourd walked to Adaleen and handed it to her.

"Another night then," she told her and rubbed her arm reassuringly. Lina then went and picked up the fish on the bank and added it to the small pile of food they had.

"This should be enough to more than stave off hunger pains," Adaleen said looking at the food. "If we ever decide to stay more than a night someplace, we will scavenge up more options," she told Lina knowing she hated having only meat. Just then, the boys returned with arms full of kindling and wood.

"Don't we need to be careful not to be seen?" Lina asked thinking about the previous night.

"That was when we were still within a stone's throw of town, here you would be hard-pressed to reach quickly on horseback and walking from the road would take hours. We should be safe," Adaleen concluded confidently as Jasper set to work, starting the fire. He got it going pretty quickly and started building a spit again while Lina cut open and cleaned the fish that Frills had caught for them. Once clean, she told Jasper she would need another spit set higher for the fish. He began putting that together as prince Dalton, covered in dirty common clothes, went to the water to wash his face. Lina busied herself putting both the rabbit and the fowl carefully on the first spit that Jasper had made, followed by the fish.

Adaleen and Jasper were by the woods looking for vantage points and blind spots from where they sat. Suddenly Lina saw them put their heads together for a moment. Soon after Jasper left, Adaleen beckoned Lina over with her hand.

"Lina, I hate to ask such a personal question but... you have stopped your blood, yes?" Adaleen asked looking at Lina waiting patiently for her answer. Lina had almost forgotten she had stopped the day before. She nodded at Adaleen who breathed a sigh of relief...

"Remember what I said about burying it deep. It will attract predators, and following the river we will have no shortage of them. The water draws in their prey, and they have to drink as well... So here." Adaleen handed Lina a stick. "You use this to count the days in between your bloods... It should always be about the same number of days... then you know when it's coming. Then you know when you have to be more careful. If it ever doesn't come when it should, tell me..." Lina turned the stick over in her hand, she wasn't sure how to use it to count. "Here," Adaleen took it and drew her knife, then notched the stick near the end, deeply so it was visible. "A notch for every day in between." Adaleen handed her back her counter and Lina went to put it in her bag. She then went to check the food, which had both boys sitting around the small fire looking famished.

"It will be done soon I think," Lina told them as she slowly rotated the spits one at a time. Frills chose this time to come out of the water and to sit by Lina. She sat with him and the prince sat opposite them.

"So I will take first watch tonight, Adaleen, you need more rest," Jasper told his sister leaving no room for argument. "Tonight we gain our strength just like Adaleen told us," Jasper said directing his word at Lina and the prince. "We can't very well keep calling you prince, should we call you Dalton?"

"That works, I... never thanked you properly... for getting me out of trouble with those men." Dalton looked sheepishly at Jasper and his sister. "Thank you, for that and allowing me to accompany you. I would have been lost if I was on my own. I didn't even know this 'River' led to the kingdom..." Dalton admitted looking grateful.

"Well, we don't know too much about you yet but we could tell you wouldn't last long out here on your own..." Adaleen looked at him with almost pity in her eyes. Lina rotated the food on the spits again and checked if they were close.

"So... what exactly happened that got you so helpless to begin with?" Jasper asked with distrust in his eyes.

"Well, I was originally surrounded when the first boom came. Then it was chaos, I was grabbed by my man and dragged back towards the manor. They were trying to get the nobles and all to seek safety in the building, which was collapsing. We saw people running to escape the roof caving inside the manor... and not making it. Then I was pushed behind my guard as they tried to get me around the building. But the people who were being herded in were all rushing towards the hill to get to town. They were pushing and running, there was screaming. The rebels started flocking them towards the cliff, people running through the fire. My guard split and some joined the fight for the field. About three men took me with the crowd around the building with great trouble as people began to reach to me begging for help. I didn't... I didn't even know where I was going or what was happening. I couldn't help anyone... My men pushed them away half dragging me towards the side of the building that was falling apart in the front after we got around the side. I think they were trying for the stables. People were streaming up from that side of the manor in waves. That's when the second boom came... The church... It engulfed the entire church... And it wasn't just fire. There were strange images in the smoke, and green-and-purple-colored sparks. The flames that grew were blue at first. It was like no fire I had ever seen, and the blast threw stone pieces through the air. I watched as people were thrown forward and crushed as people ran for their lives, clinging to children. I was thrown on the ground as I had been knocked off my feet when I realized most of the people who had been reaching for me for help had been taken out by a large stone that had been thrown. I looked to my men and one didn't move at all but laid still close by me, another had his arm broken by debris. The third stood up and turned from me. He ran away. I tried to get my legs working, but there was this loud ringing in my ear, then as people ran by me and I pulled myself to my knees, I was hit over the back of the head by something and woke up tied up with a handkerchief in my mouth."

As Dalton told the story his shoulders had slumped, he looked anguished, and horrified as he recounted the night and how it unfolded. In the end he looked as if he wished he had been another person in the story, as if his role made him feel inadequate in some way. He wouldn't meet the eyes of any of the others, but stared at the ground with clear shame on his face. Lina began taking their food off the fire to cool As Dalton looked out to the moving water.

"You couldn't have done anything..." Jasper told him certainly. "No one knew what was going to happen and now that I think about it, it seems pretty obvious. The whole of the county was practically there... and then adding you a precious member of their royal family... makes a lot of sense actually." Jasper stopped talking as Lina checked on their food and turned to Dalton.

"Do you have a preference; I know these two will eat anything," Lina asked Dalton as kindly as she could. He looked at her right in her hazel eyes and his mouth lifted into a slight smile.

"How about I'll have what you will have," he answered her, curious about her choice.

Lina took her knife and cut the rabbit in half, long ways. She then proceeded to hand the fish to Jasper, and the fowl to Adaleen. The group got silent while they ate, and Lina began to think about the story the prince had told them. She felt so sorry for his situation and what he went through. She suddenly had a rush of gratefulness for Adaleen and an appreciation for her ability to act quickly. Lina then realized... Jacob had been at the fire. She looked at Adaleen.

"Do you think Jacob made it out okay?" she asked looking at Adaleen with huge curious and hopeful eyes. Adaleen looked at Jasper and nodded.

"Jacob is strong resourceful and has more of a nose for trouble than you remember… He made it out I'm sure of it," Adaleen told her. Jasper nodded in the background and ate his fish.

"By the way, thanks Frills, this is a killer catch." Jasper tears off a bit of fish meat and throws it to where Lina and Frills sit. Frills scurries over and grabs the food then runs back to Lina to eat it.

"I'm sorry did you say 'Frills' as in you named it?" Dalton asked with a mortified expression on his face.

"Yes, Frills is with us just like you are and he joined first so I'd watch my tone if I were you," Adaleen coldly responded to Dalton.

"Okay got it, so I don't suppose we have a tent or anything right…" Dalton looked with disdain at the hard ground.

"Oh yes your majesty, we have a large size tent with a fireplace just over here for you…" Jasper mocked finishing his dinner and eyeing the tree above them for vantage points. He began to gesture and bow his way towards the woods.

"Worth a shot…" Dalton said with a smile. He looked at Lina. "Thank you for the food."

"You two will not be sleeping near each other by the way… so don't get too comfy by the fire. That's the woman's spot," Added Jasper a bit harshly.

"That's fine I'll warm up and take up over there." He pointed at a log closer to the river.

"Perfect, we can keep an eye on you..." replied Jasper not hiding his distrust. Dalton, apparently expecting this kind of treatment put his boots by the fire and held his jacket out to dry and warm.

"It's got dark quickly." Lina noted to Adaleen, who was positioning herself closer to Lina and near the fire to sleep.

"It only seems slower in town because of all the fires people have lit and the torches in the square and on some of the streets. It gets dark the same quick though. However you may notice depending on what time of year it is it may get dark sooner or later in the day," Adaleen told Lina. Lina went from sitting to laying on the soft grassy spot she had chosen. Frills scooted into her warmth and curled up. Lina curled around him and closed her eyes. She wasn't used to walking this much and was so tired that before she knew it... she fell asleep.

When Lina dreamed it was of a different forest than the one she was in. She was alone and it was dark but there were mushrooms and flowers letting off a pale glow. She noticed a small pond with a clearing in it and walked slowly towards it. She reached the pond and looked in to see there were fish that were glowing also beneath the surface. She looked at her reflection in the pond and saw herself looking back with flushed cheeks wearing a long white nightgown. Lina moved her hands along the fabric and swept her hair from her face breathing deeply. The whole place had an ethereal feel to it, and she stood back from the water and felt a breeze that made her shiver. This was not like any other dream she had had before. She felt like she could feel the soft grass beneath her feet and the nip of the wind on her skin. Lina turned and noticed a large stump. It had peculiar mushrooms growing on it and moss and plants all over. Lina moved closer and put a hand out to touch a folded up flower. As her hand got closer the flower opened and gave a low glow. Suddenly, the glow floated out of the flower and hovered up towards her. Lina thought it to be a bug that glowed. It fluttered up closer to Lina and she saw it was a bright little human with wings. It got close to her face and stopped right in front of her. Lina saw it reach a little hand out and right as it went to touch her.

"Rise and shine Lina, We got to get an early start if we are going to get to Took anytime soon." Adaleen had given Lina the smallest shake. Lina turned over and groaned... She was beginning to feel the soreness of not having a bed. Frills started stirring next to her then turned over and fell back asleep. Lina started stretching and rubbing her back then her eyes. The sun was just up from the look of it, this was an early start indeed. Jasper and Adaleen were splashing their faces in the river and pulling together their bags. Lina went to fill the gourd again and Jasper grabbed her arm.

"Lina I'd like a word with you away from prying ears later..." he mentioned casually as Dalton walked up. Still stretching and dreary eyed.

"Good idea to cover ground quickly today," he said to Jasper who looked at him with a tired drawl.

"Well Took is only a few days away, with any luck we will get there quickly and maybe even make some money for food... It's the best shot we have." Jasper looked to his sister as she stomped on and threw dirt on the fire.

"No sis like we weren't even here, you got to throw the burnt stuff and bury the whole thing." Jasper went to help his sister cover their trail a bit.

"Not easy rough campin' like this..." Dalton said politely to Lina. She smiled at him and nodded, taking a drink from the gourd and handing it to him.

"I prefer softer sleeping quarters honestly," she replied being honest and hiding from his gaze. She knew he wasn't the prince she saw in her dreams, but he is a prince and he wasn't bad looking. Just then Frills came bounding to the water and full-on jumped in leaving a huge splash in his wake. Lina giggled and Dalton smiled at her.

"He really likes you. For being someone he only just met, he seems loyal," Dalton remarked looking at her with regard.

"You said you had seen the adults before, what is he exactly?" Lina asked curiously taking back the gourd.

"He is what in the kingdom is called a Mwarlap. They are water and land-dwelling creatures, their webbed hands eventually produce much larger effective claws. He will quadruple in size, And his teeth become larger and sharper over time. They develop an upper body strength like nothing I have ever seen. They have gills hidden behind their face fins so they can stay underwater for as long as they want, they can be deadly... Having one this small would usually mean killing it before maturity, but—I have never seen one bond with a person so much. Like you're keeping him safe and he knows and respects it... maybe he thinks you're his mother or something..." He started to dismissively shake his head. Frills had dived and found a fish and was now munching on it, floating on his back.

"We won't be killing him..." Lina said certain she could and would never do that to her new friend. Frills on cue twisted in the water and swam back to Lina as she stood up. He hopped out of the water and followed her up to where the twins stood.

"We aren't having a proper breakfast," Adaleen started. "We will eat some smoked pork and more jerky until we make camp again. Lina, if you see anything worth scavenging close to the tree line, yell out one of us will take you and then we will keep moving. Make sure it is worth the stop before you say anything please," Adaleen finished looking at Lina who nodded. She understood what wasting time means. Jasper handed out the smoked pork and everyone started loading their bags onto themselves.

"I can carry a couple if you would like..." Dalton offered as the only one not carrying stuff. He reached for the gourd and Adaleen put a hand out.

"Not that," she simply stated and took the bag of meats from her brother handing it to him.

"I was also wondering, uh, if maybe I shouldn't also be armed?" He looked uncertainly at the twins. They didn't even discuss it before Jasper said,

"No, not until we decide we can trust you, which we haven't decided yet." He shook his head and continued, "Either me or Adaleen will lead, and one will follow in the back, that is how we stay safe."

Lina could see plenty of flaws in this plan but didn't say anything as they all set off again for a long day of walking and being hungry.

Much later still walking hours had gone by and Lina's feet were beginning to blister and hurt. The sun was long past its height and from the look that Dalton had on his face Lina wasn't the only one who was uncomfortable. Jasper let out a pspsp noise and Lina gratefully slowed down a bit as the others continued ahead of them.

"Say how have your dreams been lately," Jasper asked Lina looking at her intently.

"I mean how are anyone's dreams, they are mysterious to us most," Lina answered with a shrug.

"Well, how about last night did that dream seem any different than others?" Jasper asked again looking at her.

"Actually now that you mentioned it, yes it felt really real and I didn't forget it like the others," Lina recalled scratching her head. Jasper nodded and was thoughtful for a moment.

"Your mother used to have what she called waking dreams. She told Jacob about it at one point, how she would apparently jump into another place mentally and even interact with people and things, and then return to her body. It became the reason she wanted to medicate because she was starting to believe the dream world was real…" Jasper looked at Lina carefully as she considered all this information.

"She always said her back hurt from carrying the laundry," Lina said back looking unsure about the new information.

"Jacob said she started complaining about her back after your father died, before that she took it for her mind." Putting a finger to his head. "I just wonder sometimes because, you get that same look she used to…" Jasper finished looking worried.

"I haven't daydreamed in forever, and last night was the only night my dream felt like that, I'm sure it's just a coincidence," Lina finished looking at Jasper.

"As am I… but if it's all the same to you, I'd like you to tell me if any of them get too real… can you do that?" Jasper looked at Lina with concern in his eyes. She found it comforting that he cared and nodded her head.

"Thank you. Ay Adaleen," he suddenly yelled ahead of him, shading his eyes to look at the sun as it began to dip towards the trees.

"We need to stop Lina's feet are hurting, they will need to be cleaned up if she has blisters, and I have seen plenty of fish we could be getting Frills to grab."

Frills who had been following Lina on all fours bumped into her as she stopped. She turned and looked at him and he ran to the water again and dived in.

"I told you we needed to cover ground today." Adaleen had stalked back to where her brother and Lina were.

"We have in the last couple, I can already see the smokestacks for Took over the trees Just there we need to let everyone rest up, Lina isn't the only one who looks tired..." He nodded in the direction of the prince.

"I'm sorry don't stop because of me, I will keep up... just not terribly used to walking this much and eating so little," Dalton explained, with a reassuring tone, though he sat immediately and wiped sweat from his forehead.

"Well fine I'm hungry and tired then," Jasper said, finally setting down his bags. "Besides, Lina can scavenge over there after she rests her feet and checks the blisters..." He nodded towards the opening to the woods where a tree stump with mushrooms was peeking out.

"Well, all right fine, I hadn't realized we got so close. Well, it actually makes sense with following the river." Adaleen set down her bag and took Lina's. Jasper started handing out salted jerky to the group.

"Uhh, I'm so hungry," the prince said as he wolfed down his own bit of Jerky. Lina nibbled on hers and waited for frills who came up after a moment and set a fish down by her. She set down a piece of the Jerky as thanks.

"Frills..." Jasper began pointing at the Jerky then pointing at the fish, trying to communicate with him. "You give me fish, I give you jerky," He started pointing at Frills, then the fish, then himself, then the jerky. Frills looked at him not understanding then looked down at the fish and suddenly ran back to the water.

"You will never get him to get it…" Adaleen said as he came back up with another fish earning another little piece of jerky.

"I can try though…" Jasper set to work making the same movements and looking meaningfully at Frills. Adaleen rolled her eyes and mentioned something about wood stalking off to the forest.

"I think he gets it…" Jasper said as Frills again ran to the river and dived in.

"I never even realized they could understand people before." Dalton looked on in amusement. "He is practically trainable."

"That he is…" Jasper noted as he again broke the surface of the water with yet another fish. This time Frills set the fish down and turned, waiting for his treat. Jasper bent down and handed him the jerky saying, 'just one more'. He again pointed from Frills to the fish then to the jerky and himself as Frills chewed. He ran back to the water and dived yet again.

"Well if I didn't know any better I'd say he understands you…" said Lina looking amused by the whole scene as she pulled her boots from her feet.

"Kindred spirits, the two of us…" Jasper mentioned quietly picking up the gourd and taking drink. Lina wondered what he meant by that just as Adaleen showed up with an armful of sticks and kindling to start a fire.

"Lina, would you clean the fish please, I would but Jasper has a fit when I touch the food…"

"That because things become inedible when you touch them…" Jasper responded getting a stick thrown in his direction for the cheek.

"Here he comes again…" Dalton watched as Frills climbed the side of the river to drop the fourth fish again by Lina. "Amazing, I have never seen a Mwarlap do anything for a person… usually they just attack them."

"I'm sure it's more self-defense than attack…" Adaleen looked at him coldly as she said this.

"Uh, are we really that close to town?" Dalton mentioned pointing at the smoke over the trees a way up.

"We made pretty good time so yea, not gunna have to tie you up are we?" Adaleen asked looking happy to do so. Lina watched him turn a little red as he explained he had nowhere to go to her.

"I'm just happy to be traveling with what appears is decent company, I owe you two a lot," Dalton tried saying to appease the twins…

"And I guess Lina and Frills are just your entertainment…" Jasper barked pushing him towards the water. "Go soak your feet Prince… can't have you getting an infection and losing a leg…"

"Lina and Frills are the best part of this trip, don't mistake me, I am grateful to have people who are smart and know how to travel like you two, but Lina and Frills, make this whole thing much more bearable." He sat at the edge of the water.

Lina cleaned the fish as Adaleen prepped the fire for dinner. Jasper laid in the ditch near the water on the tall grass while the prince dipped his feet and winced every now and again.

"Lina you will have to dip yours too with the way they look," Adaleen told Lina. She nodded as she started skewering the fish and carefully put them on the fire.

"So tomorrow Took, next week Mareep. We should be able to stop and get some supplies. We will work it all out tomorrow, for now, let's rest up and get ready to enjoy a nice night with full bellies," Jasper said lying down comfortably in the ditch. He stretched an arm behind his head and closed his eyes. It was a long day, and the group was quiet as they all started thinking of the first stop in their journey. Took was a town of hunters and traders, with the occasional mercenary in the shadows... surely the knowledge of what happened in Crestfallen village had reached them... but maybe not. They each relaxed for the first time all day, as Jasper started to nap in the grass, he had easily slept the least over the trip, so nobody woke him as they waited for the fish to cook. Frills went and sniffed him and curled up at his side while the smoke from the fire rose into the subtly darkening sky.

Chapter 9

The next morning Lina rose to find Jasper awake again. He had just started building a fire. Adaleen and Dalton were still fast asleep. Lina went to the water to wash her feet and fill the gourd. She then saw Frills lying on a rock snoring away. She looked at Jasper for a moment and then through the clearing where there was clearly mushrooms and herbs that could be scavenged.

"Would you walk me over to the clearing just there?" Lina asked Jasper pointing in-between the trees.

"Yea sure ought to let these two sleep a bit more." Jasper and Lina walked through the trees with Lina's bag to look around for mushrooms and herbs.

"I haven't seen many animals, birds or anything…" Jasper noted looking around after catching sight of a berry bush. He started nibbling on the berries on the top branches that looked ripe.

"Took is a big hunting town… animals have probably gotten a sense to not get too close," Lina told him thinking about what her father used to say.

She had a sudden flash back of him telling Jacob "Animals don't go to where hunters are, so hunters have to go to where animals are." She smiled to herself as she stooped to pick another mushroom. Lina grabbed about half a bag full of mushrooms, a few different herbs and a few handfuls of the berries before heading back to the camp. Once at the camp, she could see Adaleen had woken and Frills was licking Dalton's feet.

"Where were you two off to then?" Adaleen asked with a huge yawn and stretch. Lina handed her the bag of mushrooms and herbs and showed her the berries.

"All right, I think I have had enough fish for the year. Ay, wakey wakey..." Adaleen threw a rock towards Dalton which startled him awake.

"We got a little grub and it's time to make a plan," Adaleen said as he rose and started stretching also. Dalton went to the water and all but stuck his face in it splashing himself awake.

"I never thought I'd say this, but I think I'm getting used to sleeping on the ground," Dalton joked as he walked towards the fire and sat with the others. Frills, who no longer had feet to lick ran forward and dived into the water. Popping back up and blowing a stream of water straight into the air.

"All right... this is what we have for food... plus, Jasper any more smoked or salted meat left?"

"Little smoked venison not even enough to feed us alone though," Jasper answered looking in his bag.

"That means we need to be able to hunt unless we want to live off fish or starve. I think the best idea is to get a bow, me and Jasper are good if the prince can use one it's an easier call..." Adaleen looked to Dalton hopeful that he had some experience.

"Uh, to be honest I always preferred classes on swordplay than shooting..." He looked a little red at this, realizing his skills has fallen short of useful thus far.

"Well we can't get a sword, not at a good price here... Me and Jasper can handle the hunting then. We need a better hooded cloak for you I think also... What else could we use do you think for the trip... other than food and booze, Jasper..." Jasper had raised his hand then dropped it quickly.

"Maybe we should get a cart... then we could carry more," said Dalton trying to be helpful...

"That's on the right track but traveling along the river the terrain is too unpredictable, we could get stuck or break a wheel too easy, anything else?" Adaleen stopped again and looked around at everyone who looked back at her tired and hungry.

"A bed for a night wouldn't be a terrible idea..." mentioned Lina looking off at the water and watching Frills.

"Yea about that... Lina I don't know about you or Dalton going into town... Hear me out, people have almost definitely heard about the prince being missing which is why we can't have him go, but you having Frills is going to draw unwanted attention, people just don't keep pets like him..." Adaleen tried sincerely to sound objective.

"So I can't even go with?" Lina asked sorely.

"I'm afraid I agree with Adaleen, Its too risky without knowing how things are right off, people could be paranoid we are rebel scouts, I think it's best you hang back..." He eyed Dalton as he told Lina this to see a reaction. If Dalton gave any, Jasper gave no sign.

"Will you be selling the rings; we could probably get a proper carriage for the price of two much less all four..." Dalton said hopefully. The twins looked at each other before bursting into laughter...

"We will be getting the thieves price and be lucky if they ask us no questions," replied Jasper wiping a tear from his eye.

"A proper carriage, it's not like we can say you gave it to us and take it to a respectable jewelry shop..." Adaleen hiccupped from laughing so hard. Dalton turned rather red again.

"Oh yea I guess that makes sense..." He picked up a mushroom and nibbled on it clearly no longer wishing to help. Adaleen noticing the deflated egos of Dalton and Lina thought a moment.

"How about this, we stay here a day or two... me and Jasper get what we can for the rings, get the supplies and some food and come back here. Then we can hunt a couple days and sell whatever we pull in and don't have to eat. We might even be able to get a trap or two... Then if we make enough, the last night we sneak you three into town and get a room so everyone can get a full night's sleep before we take off again. Mareep is a lot longer walk than Took was. How does that sound?"

"That sounds good," Lina said excited to relax and possibly sleep in a bed. Dalton suddenly lit up.

"A net... we could pull in all the fish we need, or enough rope I can tie one together..." he said suddenly working his hands in a strange pattern.

"Okay a net is a great idea; we will see what we can find," Adaleen assured him.

"Are we sure about leaving the two of them?" Jasper asked Adaleen again eyeing Dalton who was suddenly busy fixing his boot.

"I have a feeling he knows we will hunt him down without sleep if he touches her, so yea I'm sure," Adaleen said clearly in a threatening tone. Adaleen grabbed a few mushrooms and shoved them in her mouth chewing furiously.

"Mm, these are pretty good," she said throwing one at Jasper who caught it and ate it.

"If we hurry and go, we could be back just after midday. Maybe we could get some kind of pot to cook with..." Adaleen stood and stretched as Jasper pulled the last of the smoked venison out of his bag and divide it up. He then ate a single berry and asked for the gourd.

"All right well... Lina you keep hold of your knife... better you have it than him. We will be back, you will just have to wait for us, all right," Jasper said mostly to Lina as Dalton picked through the berries.

"Okay I'm sure you won't be too long." Lina looked at Jasper and smiled reassuringly. The twins stayed and finished filling their bellies with the fungi and pocketed the smoked venison they had portioned for themselves. Lina saw Adaleen take the rings out of a bag and stuff them in her jacket out of sight. Then take the empty bags they had and put them in a single bag to carry. Jasper walked over to Dalton and started talking to him in a hushed voice. Dalton nodded a couple of times but said nothing and looked unconcerned from what Lina could tell. Then the twins grabbed their things and set off hiking towards the smoke pillars over the trees.

Lina and Dalton watched as the river's edge twisted, and they followed it out of sight. Frills jumped out of the water and looked at Lina then looked after Adaleen and Jasper.

"Don't worry they will be back," Lina said to him scooping him into her arms and running a finger along his spine. Lina turned and saw Dalton sitting by the fire staring into it.

"May I ask, what did Jasper say before he left?" She looked at him inquiringly hoping it wasn't another vague threat to protect her from him.

"Just asked me to find wood and feed the fire so it didn't go out, then he told me not to leave you alone for too long, and to make sure I keep an eye on you both, he said it was important, the most important job on this trip..." he answered looking towards the woods and nibbling on another mushroom. "I have to be honest, I'm hungry so I can't not eat it but these taste like dirt... do you eat them often?" He held a mushroom up to Lina.

"My mother said mushrooms are important because they are good for us and keep us grounded... before she got sick..." Lina responded looking at Dalton daring him to meet her eyes.

"I don't know that I had ever had one before now. I never paid attention to what was in my food really..." Dalton admitted with a smile. "Never in all my years did I think I would be in this situation though, or I might have brushed up fire building, shelter making and food hunting skills." He looked over at Lina with amusement on his face and they both laughed at his lack of preparation.

"It was truly lucky that I ended up with you three. I'm grateful. Also I believe Jasper is right, keeping you safe is the most important thing they have tasked me with, and I mean to however." Dalton looked up at the sky back down towards the water. "I haven't bathed in days so if you don't mind, I will be getting in the water." He began walking to the bank and started taking his shirt off. He sat on a rock and took his boots off then the pants. Standing stark naked a moment he faced the water.

"Hope it's not too cold... arghghgh..." Frills had jumped in splashing Dalton with water. Dalton jumped in after as Lina laughed trying to look away for his privacy.

"It's actually quite nice in here... If you want to get in, I can turn around... it's up to you..." Dalton started swimming around and dunked his head under the water. Lina considered the offer and thought about how she hadn't properly cleaned herself in days, including when her blood was ending. Lina went to the bank and found another rock close to the water she could set her stuff on. She looked at Dalton who was losing a race with Frills in the water. Lina took off her jacket and sat to remove her boots. Her feet still didn't look the best it was probably good they were waiting a few days she thought to herself. She looked again and saw that Dalton was busy giving her space as she removed her sheath and necklace. She started to unfasten and slide her pants off, the long shirt Adaleen had given her covered her down to her knees almost, but she took off the shirt and laid it down next to the rock. She positioned her sheath and knife, so it was easy for her to see it from the water, then turned and looked at Dalton. She took a huge breath and jumped in.

The water was cool but felt good as the sun was warming it up. Lina shivered a moment as she swam the length of the river and back quickly. Frills came up to her with a snake he had caught and killed in his mouth. He floated on his back, and she rubbed his tummy. He cooed and swam towards Dalton who was staring slightly mesmerized by Lina. He shook his head and apologized and asked if she needed help taking her hair down later. Lina raised her hand and felt the braid in her hair that was coming apart slightly and seemed messy.

"Adaleen can take it out tonight and I can rinse my hair again," she answered him with a smile, swimming over to him "This was a good idea... it feels good in here."

"It does but I actually think I should get out... Dalton looked away from Lina and she saw color rising on his cheeks, she looked down and saw the water wasn't entirely transparent but could slightly be seen through. "I'm good anyway, we wouldn't want anyone sneaking up on us while we are in here, you go ahead and soak for a bit and have fun." Dalton started to swim to the bank where his clothes were and pulled himself out of the water. Lina being curious didn't look away, she dipped her head so nothing but her eyes and nose were out of the water and watched the prince as he pulled his pants on, then continued swimming giggling to herself about what she saw. Lina swam back and forth and raced with Frills a few times who always won before heading to her rock where her sheath is.

"I'm gunna get out," Lina called up to Dalton as Frills climbed the bank next to her.

"Go ahead I'm throwing some wood on the fire," she heard him respond from over the bank. She climbed out on the dry reeds and grass and up to her rock with her clothing. When Lina got out, she looked at herself and noted her body had still been changing, her hips slightly wider and her breast slightly fuller. The clothes were still dirty, but she pulled them on regardless, feeling better about being clean herself. She bent over to grab her shirt and caught a glimpse of the prince staring at a nearby tree. Though she could swear she felt his eyes wandering towards her she pulled the shirt on and tucked it into the pants. Both were pretty baggy on her. She then picked up the sheath… and slung it around her waist after fastening the pants up. She balled up her Jacket and went to set it down by the fire, and felt up to her braid again, sure it looked wild and untidy from the days of wearing it.

"Please let me help..." Dalton said as Lina sat down. He moved from his spot to behind her and knelt down over her. "My little sister *hates* braids... every time my mother has her hair done that way she whines and pouts because she says it hurts her head. They pull them very tight you see..." The prince took the bottom of the braid with the dirty ribbon in his hand and began expertly unworking it. "So every time she gets them put in she waits for the opportunity and runs to me wherever I am, and asks me to take them out." He continued working his way up the braid working quickly and accurately as if he knew exactly where to pull. "I never made her cry or beg or ask more than once, I would sit her down and take it out." He told her as he began unfurling the top of the braid from her head pulling out the ribbon and dropping it to the side. Lina liked the feel of his hands in her hair and imagined a little girl crying to him and him taking her hair down. "I always told her, she looks best happy, hair done or not." He finished his little story as the last bits of Lina's hair came out.

"I knew you had a little sister and brother but I don't know how old they are..." Lina admitted pushing her fingers through her hair as Dalton walked around her side and sat at the fire.

"They are both young Anabelle is only four she is as bright as the sun some days, but throws a tantrum like a god. And Quentin is five, he has been reading a lot lately. Spends time in the library even when classes are done, he seems to enjoy it. I miss them, they are my favorite people in the whole world." He concluded looking a little sad for a moment. Lina knew the feeling, she felt like with Jacob gone, part of her was missing.

"You will see them again," she told him as reassuringly as she could. She stretched a little and stifled a yawn.

"Do you want to rest? The twins haven't had me on guard duty so I can stay up if you want to," Dalton asked Lina as he stood and walked to the small pile of wood and found a stick to prod the fire with. Lina considered the offer and realized she was still tired, lately she hadn't been sleeping as well at night. The nights she slept through she woke up still tired. She smiled and agreed to lay down for a bit.

Lina lay down and closed her eyes and instantly began sleeping. She had a dream she was climbing a mountain but whoever she was with was higher above than her. She tried to see the top bout couldn't and looked down and everything was disappearing. There was some sort of void or darkness that was advancing slowly up the mountain. Lina yelled out frightened and tried to climb. She moved her hands and worked her arms but for some reason she seemed to not be getting anywhere, suddenly Adaleen was over her reaching a hand out and yelling to come on, to hurry. Lina reached for her hand but couldn't reach it and kept trying to climb but kept getting nowhere. She felt the dark void advancing and knew she would be swallowed up when she slipped, and slowly started falling backwards. She saw a look of terror on Adaleen's face as she fell and saw the darkness surround her as she kept falling then…

Lina was startled awake by something heavy landing on her. she opened her eyes and saw a man was there holding her down. The sun was high in the sky, and she started struggling as he pinned her arms up by her head.

"And what is this. Little rebel girl out in the woods alone… not very smart…" Lina screamed and struggled.

"That's enough girl…" the man raised a hand and slapped Lina. "No one's coming to save you…" He started pulling at Lina's shirt. She began to beg and plead with him…

"No please, please let me go…" She struggled against his heavy hand that held both her dainty wrist above her. "Noo let me goo… Help" She was smacked again. This time making her a little dazed.

"I said stop that…" His hand yanked at her shirt ripping it slightly and traveled down towards her waist. Lina felt fear, a shiver flowed through her body she closed her eyes, her heart began to race as a warm filled her chest, it spread through her and up into her arms.

"Ow… what… " the man pulled his hand away from her wrists and pulled back slightly…

Thud. The pressure slid off of Lina…

Thud, thud, thud, thud suddenly the sound of something cracking *Thud…

"Lina… Lina are you okay… oh my God Lina." She opened her eyes and saw two silhouettes lining up in her eye sight. The sun glared down behind Dalton as he leaned forward and stretched out a hand to help her up. "Lina I'm so sorry I was gone for only a moment with Frills to grab more wood… I swear I didn't hear anyone coming… I'm so sorry this is my fault…" Lina looked to her side and saw that the man who was rather large and ugly was bleeding profusely from the crack that Dalton had just put in his head with a rather large rock.

Lina touched her head where she had been hit and felt a small bump and bruise forming. She suddenly began understanding the situation and how close that was to being worse and reached out and hugged Dalton with tears in her eyes.

"Thank you, thank you so much…" Lina didn't know much about what he was trying to do to her but she knew it wasn't something she wanted him doing. She had never felt so disgusted in her life after being touched like that. She was nothing but glad that Dalton had been there to save her.

"Ohhh, Jasper might kill me… Maybe if I hide him?" He seemed to be asking himself more than anything. Lina put her hand to her eyes and looked up.

"No time it's midday already," she told him pointing at the sun. "No, better to just tell the truth, you didn't do anything wrong, you had to have only been gone a moment. and they told you to look after the fire…" She pointed out. "Plus, thanks to you, I'm fine…" she finished and looked at Dalton with admiration. "And you didn't even have a proper weapon, even Adaleen has to respect that a little…"

Dalton kicked the man on the ground to make sure he wasn't moving. He seemed to be dead, he seemed to be thinking hard about what she had said, trying to decide if he was still safe with the twins after his lapse in protection. He seemed to decide to stay and sat down hanging his head slightly.

"I shouldn't have left..." he said looking at the ground.

"Actually he shouldn't have bothered me. He wasn't a good person..." Lina said sitting by him and putting a hand on his shoulder. She suddenly had an idea and smiled. "When I become queen, all men who hurt woman or children will be put all together in a town and not allowed to leave it." She joked looking at him. Dalton looked at her questioningly.

"It's like a game... My dad called me princess Lina once so me and Adaleen used to pretend, I was royalty when I was little, as I got older, we played less but would still make royal decrees up for fun," she told him with a smile. Dalton smiled and considered her, then started grinning.

"That's actually adorable. The idea isn't sustainable though, you couldn't guarantee that no woman or children venture into the town... It would be too dangerous for anyone outside it..." he said to her laughing at her idea. "You would have to have them watched and locked in a giant dungeon... Maybe just a building of dungeon cells..." he said to her thinking himself on the idea. Lina thought about this addition and realized he was right, and his idea was better.

"I mean for people who are dangerous though... that's not a terrible idea..." he told her. They sat for a while in silence with a man's dead body nearby. Lina had to stop Frills from gnawing on it three times but he was back to the water blowing bubbles and diving for fish when all of a sudden...

"And what in the ever-loving hell is that body doing there..." came Jasper's voice from off in the distance.

"Well if they are going to kill me, we will know soon," Dalton said standing up with Lina and Jasper and Adaleen started running towards camp. They ran quickly and reached the camp faster than Lina would have thought possible... As soon as they arrived, they started looking around wildly and catching their breath. Lina saw that Adaleen carried a nice bow and a quick with arrows now.

"Who... What... start talking..." said Adaleen frustrated and trying to breathe... Lina tried to start explaining but was cut off flat out by Dalton.

"It's my fault. you told me not to leave her alone and I thought I could take a minute to grab fire wood, Frills followed me. Someone showed up while I was in the wood and I heard the struggle and her yell out, I got back as fast as I could..." Dalton finished looking ashamed of himself and refusing to look anyone in the eye. Adaleen walked up to Lina...

"He didn't." Adaleen turned pale. "... He didn't touch you did he.?" Lina was embarrassed but told her what happened from her side.

"I woke up to him holding me down, he smacked me a few times and groped beneath my shirt and tore it but almost immediately Dalton showed up and beat him over the head..." Adaleen checked Lina's cheek and looked her over thoroughly to make sure she was okay.

Jasper who hadn't said anything this entire time but sat back and watched everyone's reactions walked up to Dalton finally. Dalton, looking worried, slowly brought his eyes up to meet Jasper's. Jasper slowly took a bag he had been carrying off and held it in his hand, letting his arm fall to its side. They stared at each other for a moment, Jasper unreadable and Dalton concerned. Jasper thrusted the bag out to Dalton and said,

"All right, now I trust you." With a wide smile on his face. "You did good..." he said with a nod of approval and Dalton took the bag from him with an obvious sigh of relief. "What's wrong buddy, you act like I was going to kill you..." Jasper said laughing at the end as if it was the most clever joke.

"We were starting to already, but this does push you past the line. We don't need you to kill for us, but If you're willing to protect Lina there can be no denying you are now part of this group," Adaleen added turning from Lina and going up to Dalton. She gave him a brief hug and said thank you.

"Well now that that is all out in the open, we should move this body so it isn't..." Jasper said to Dalton. "Here, eat this quick and we will move this while Lina cooks us some meat." Jasper threw some bread to both Lina and Dalton then went to set his bags down. Lina and Dalton ate the bread fairly quickly, grabbed a drink each, then set to their different tasks. The boys dragged the body into the woods somewhere and were gone the whole time Lina cooked and came back covered in dirt and mud. Adaleen had given Lina three rabbits to roast and a pan for the various vegetables she had gotten.

Lina used the herbs she had grabbed earlier and cooked the meat to perfection, she wanted to make it as perfect as possible for her savior. She added a little water to the vegetables to soften them as they cooked in the pan on top of some embers. The boys came back and went to wash up as she pulled the spit down full of rabbits. Adaleen asked what they did with the man, and Lina heard them talk about stripping it of anything worthwhile before tuning into her cooking. She did not want to think about the man or what would have happened if Dalton hadn't showed up. She decided to focus on her thank you. Which was the most delicious meal she had been able to serve so far: herb roasted rabbit and fresh roasted potatoes. The twins had more bread and Jasper even got Adaleen to let him get some wine.

They sat all their food in a pile once it was all finished and sat together. Jasper reached out and grabbed the first Rabbit's leg and the wine he had just opened.

"I say the first bite from now on should go to the hero of the day." Jasper handed both the rabbit leg and the wine to Dalton who smiled and looked at Jasper as if he were his brother.

"Thank you. For the record, I'm just glad you're okay." Dalton looked at Lina for a moment.

"Yes yes, take the bite I'm still hungry!" Jasper urged him. Dalton took a bite of the rabbit and looked blissful to have such good hot food, he then swigged the wine and handed both to Lina.

"I say the second goes to Lina, for being worth fighting for," Dalton said to whoops and cheers from the twins. Lina blushed and took the food and wine, took a small bite and a tiny drink that made her cough and sputter for the unexpected taste.

"All right let's dig in shall we…" Adaleen told her brother as they all dived their hands towards random food and drink. Frills came out of the water and sat next to Lina. She gave him the leg to gnaw on and patted his smooth head while munching on the bread. It was a close call with a good ending and she couldn't help but replay what Dalton had said about her over and over in her head. She thought about it well into the night, as the laughter died down as the fire grew small and the sky dark. She thought about it before she went to sleep, he thought she was worth fighting for… was the last thing she thought about as she was whisked away to dream.

Chapter 10

The next morning Lina woke to the sound of a hard thud followed by hushed voices. She squeezed her eyes closed and tried to listen to who was talking. She heard Jasper whispering to Dalton, and Dalton replying before she heard another soft thud. Lina yawned and stretched and finally decided to open her eyes. She turned towards the noise and half rolled over Frills who had been curled up next to her.

"Umpff..." Frills jumped up and ran up to lick her face. She started to giggle as she tried to pull Frills away. His face split into a wide yawn and he stretched his little legs and arms. Lina turned towards the boys and saw Jasper showing Dalton how to throw a knife into a tree.

"You almost got it, oh hey, Lina is up! Adaleen should be back soon she went to hunt a little early this morning," Jasper said no longer hiding his voice. Dalton gave Lina a smile and walked over to where the gourd sat, picking it up. He brought it over to Lina who sat up and took a drink of the water.

"We have to map out our next move once Adaleen gets back, we have things to talk about from town and supplies to go over," Jasper told Lina. Lina went over to the food they had made the previous night and picked up the pan Adaleen had gotten her. She walked towards the river and began rinsing it out. She then set the pan down to go to the woods to relieve herself. As she walked towards the woods Jasper yelled out not to go far in and threw a knife expertly at the x marked on the tree in front of him while Dalton watched.

Lina went into the woods to pee and Frills followed her closely sniffing random things at her feet and running around trees. She couldn't figure out if he preferred all fours or two legs as he frequently stood and moved both ways. She relieved herself and was fastening her pants back up when she heard a growl coming from Frills. She turned to look at him and saw he was staring off at the trees a bit away where there was a silhouette of a man. Lina suddenly felt fear, she grabbed for her blade and called out for Jasper in a shaky voice, remembering the man on top of her.

Both boys came bounding through the trees in a moment, knives raised and looking for the trouble.

"Lina what is it?" Jasper asked not seeing anything. Lina pointed in the direction Frills had been growling in, but the silhouette was gone.

"There was a man there I think…" she said suddenly unsure of herself. "It could have been a weird shadow or a trick of the light, but she could have sworn she saw a hard outline…"

"Hmm, well if there was someone there, he got scared off quickly…" Jasper said as he and Dalton lowered their knives. "I'm gunna go look for fresh tracks Dalton can you take her back to the river?" Dalton put his knife away and ushered Lina back to the water.

"What's all this then?" Adaleen had just returned to the camp with what looked like two fat beavers.

She sat down and started to gut them throwing the guts across the river. Lina watched as the blood started spilling out. She didn't mind blood any more, she wouldn't feel sick of queasy looking at it.

"I saw someone in the woods... I thought... Jasper went to check it out," Lina told Adaleen looking sorry.

"Well if there was anyone there, he would see something. Let's not worry until we know something. Dalton, do you know how to gut animals?" she asked looking skeptically at the young prince.

"I can't say that I do," he said already watching with interest.

"Well here, it's time you learn. All right so to skin it we are going to cut the fur up off the skin, here, here, here and here." Adaleen starts pulling the skin off the beaver meat and yanks it down to the tail. Then shows him how to gut the next one and lets him pull the skin off himself. He did good other than looking slightly green.

"You're a quick study," Adaleen told him in the end handing the beavers to Lina. She then went and started looking at the multiple bags they had as Jasper walked up to the camp.

"Oooh, you found something great!" he replied clapping his hands together and rubbing them as Lina skewered the beaver on the spit.

"I'm much more interested in what you found," replied Adaleen, looking on patiently at her brother.

"Well, no tracks or broken branches or twigs, no disturbed plants or paths, honestly it didn't look like anyone had been there, probably just a trick of the light at a vulnerable moment," Jasper concluded.

"Okay either way I think it's important every one of us keeps an eye and an ear out..." Adaleen looked wearily at the woods, then back to her brother. "We need to talk plan and supplies. We didn't get around to it yesterday with everything that happened but we can't put it off any more. Dalton," Adaleen regarded Dalton and he gave her his attention. "Everyone knows you're missing, and the king has put out a huge reward for you... All of the hunters and mercs showed interest so..." Adaleen dug in a bag and pulled out a cloak. "We need to keep you hidden at all costs. Also, we are going to skip this town and get a bed in Mareep. There are less people interested and capable of taking you there. Maybe by the time we arrive, the buzz of it all will die down, but apparently Crestfallen village being burned has caused a stir through the kingdom." Adaleen looked at Jasper who picked up where she left off.

"There weren't as many casualties as we thought but everybody lost everything, the whole village was burned down. All the survivors left to seek asylum in the closest towns or with people they knew elsewhere, but now everyone is worried that they might be next. People are being called into question for activity, guards are not allowing people in places and towns, it's getting ugly. We think it would be best If we avoid most towns if we can, and stay away from people. We already know we can't trust the guards working for the crown, everyone is apparently suspect." Jasper finished reaching into his bag pulled out a rope. "We were able to get you a net but I don't know how much luck you will have with it until we find a resting pond on the side of the river." Jasper handed the bag with the rope to Dalton who nodded and threw it over his shoulder.

At that point, Adaleen pulled out a map they had also apparently gotten of the kingdom. She and Jasper and Dalton bent their heads over it talking about the path and how to shorten their trip. Dalton seemed to know a lot about the different areas and what kind of problems they could face in them, also what kind of dangerous people and animals there were. Lina watched him while she turned their food with a smile, he seemed happy to be able to contribute. They talked about setting a path most of the time Lina cooked. She didn't make any vegetables as she decided meat and bread would be enough for a hearty breakfast as the other three went through the supplies.

"Extra gourds were smart." Dalton noted as he looked at the three new gourds for them each to carry.

"Figure after we looked at the map, we might part from the river a bit," Jasper answered with a smile. "You know you guys barely touched the wine last night I have half a bottle still." He held up the red wine and shook it.

"We saved it for you as you're not going to be getting any more for a long while," Adaleen said with a stern look on her face.

"that's fair I suppose," Jasper said opening the bottle and taking a decent sized swig, he then handed the bottle to Dalton who took a small bit and wiped his mouth.

"I'll have to give you wine when we reach the castle, I'm telling you you have never tasted anything so sweet..." Dalton told Jasper with a smile. Lina pulled the meat off the fire to cool as it was finally cooked.

"I'll be holding you to that..." Jasper said as they continued dispersing supplies in specific bags and separating things for each of them. Lina started stoking the fire and decided to add a log or two. She went to the pile and grabbed a few and when she stood up just past the tree line it was like a dark shadow was there. It didn't seem to be solid, like just an outline of a person, but Lina just stared.

"You need help?" Adaleen asked walking over by Lina and taking the wood from her. Lina looked back and the shadow was gone.

"Thank you," Lina responded certain she didn't want to alarm them over nothing again.

The boys sat down, and they all started tearing into the beaver and bread and talking about packing up to move on the next morning. They had decided to go around the business side of Took. They would stay far enough back in the forest that they couldn't be detected and once they moved a way past the town they would make their way back to the river.

"It's not like we could get turned around with this guy with us," Jasper said throwing a piece of meat in the air for Frills to jump up and catch. The plan sounded solid and they sat and enjoyed the morning together. Around midday Jasper and Dalton decided to give hunting a try, see if they could catch something small for dinner.

"All the bigger game must be more in the woods, I didn't know there were a couple ponds they could get water from out there." Adaleen told Lina complaining about the lack of bigger game.

"Maybe we will get lucky, and they will find something, should we keep pelts, you think?" she asked Lina absent-mindedly. holding up an uncleansed beaver pelt. She started muttering prices for things in town and cast them aside. "I think it's more worth selling the meat, and way less trouble." She made the decision without a word from Lina who nodded in agreement. "You handle blood better I noticed…" Adaleen started and looked to Lina curiously.

"Everything bleeds, I guess it isn't as strange to me now…" Lina said thinking of her first blood. But it was more than that. Lina knew that at the point that the prince was saved, she didn't barely notice the blood, when Jasper was saved before that the same. Almost as if she just stopped seeing it the same way. Good blood and bad blood, She didn't see any reason to cry or get sick over spilled bad blood she just hadn't realized it till now.

"Well we need to take a swim, or our scent alone will be enough to bring in all the predators," she said looking at Lina. "I meant to ask, how did you get the braid out."

"Dalton took it out for me, and actually." Lina looked away a little embarrassed. "Me and Dalton took a swim when you and Jasper left. We kept our distance, and he was a complete gentleman, but it was nice." She finished watching Adaleen take in the information.

"Oh you went for a swim huh? Well at least you got yourself cleaned up... At some point we will get spare clothes so we can wash and switch but for now we will have to stay strong with what we have... so did you... see anything while you were swimming." Lina turned so red she didn't even have to answer. Adaleen started laughing like mad.

"We will have to have a talk while the boys are gone then... after yesterday I need you to know what I have been easing into talking to you about, and what me Jacob and Jasper have been trying to protect you from... Come here Lina it's time you finally hear about sex..." Lina went and settled in by Adaleen wondering what she was talking about. Adaleen sipped the wine Jasper had left as the fire crackled and they sat down for a long talk about woman's and men's bodies and consent.

The boys returned before sundown with a large goose and a couple of rabbits. The girls, having gone through many giggling fits and awkward explanations, were sitting back eating berries and smiling back and forth. Adaleen got up to add more wood to the fire and Lina stood to stretch. The boys started cleaning their catches and Lina heard them talking about none other than her father.

"We learned from the best, honest hand to God. Lina's dad was the best hunter and trapper around. He even sold to the king once before."

"Huh that's actually funny my dad mentioned having a top hunter years before they could catch and kill anything. I wonder if Lina's dad would have been better than the hunter Gerald."

"Wait, but that's what his name was, Gerald," Jasper said taken a back.

"Weird well my dad's great hunter disappeared after going to the forbidden east on a hunting trip like thirty years ago. He still shows people the pelts of the amazing creatures and animals that Gerald hunted down. He died doing what he loved though." Dalton finished and suddenly looked up curiously.

"We should keep our bags hidden but in one location so if we have to leave in the middle of the night, we can move quickly but also if our camp is spotted it would be harder to take our stuff," said Jasper looking at all the bags. They would easily be carrying two each plus a gourd. Lina's legs ached a little just thinking about it, but then she pictured Jacob at the base of the waterfall and she felt better. She was going to find him no matter what it took. Jasper brought the rabbits to Lina and set the goose to the side on a rock. Lina skewered the rabbits and stuffed their mouths and chest cavities with herbs, then put them high over the fire. She planned to manually turn them so they would cook even and taste a little like smoked meat. Adaleen Jasper and Dalton sat around the fire as the sun sunk towards the trees. Dalton looked uneasy like he was struggling with something. Jasper was explaining the first time he got a kill throwing a knife at small game near him and the feeling he got. He said Gerald had never looked so proud. Lina and Adaleen were smiling when Dalton cleared his throat.

"I have been wondering but haven't known how to ask..." he started looking at Jasper unsure if he was overstepping.

"Well you will be hard pressed to find anything out if you don't do what you have to for the information..." Jasper said. As he said it, the smile slipped from his face. "You want to know about our parents." He looked at Adaleen who held a long look with him. They seemed to be talking to each other again without a single visible que.

"If it's too much for me to ask, then forget about it, I just feel like I'm getting to know you guys and I have had some questions is all, like well that topic, I guess..." Dalton cut off looking away and rubbing the back of his neck. He was clearly uncomfortable asking for such personal information, even from someone he is getting on with as well as Jasper.

"There isn't much to tell. They went to Took with their carriage to make sales one day. Our father was a Lumberer. He and Ma asked Gerald to look in and feed us while they were gone. They didn't come back. We never knew if they left or if something happened, but that last hug and kiss from Ma, and Pa saying to be good, was it?" Jasper looked back at Adaleen who knew where the conversation was going apparently and looked hard at the ground.

"After about six days and nights Gerald got worried and took us into town to make a report, thinking the king's guards in town could maybe check the road or at least send word to see if they ever made it there. He walked us in and talked to the town's head of the guard. The man was a drunk and looked shady, Gerald asked him what he would do, and he said he had to leave us there. That he would find the parents or send us to an orphanage, but he did the right thing by taking us... there..." Jasper stopped and looked again at his sister who refused to meet his eyes and had the occasional tear streaming down her face. Lina slowly turned the rabbit and listened to the story; she had never heard before. She only ever knew they went to the market and didn't return.

"We were only about four maybe five, and Gerald didn't like the way he was looking at us but the man started yelling he was in charge of the guard, and he was to take care of these problems. They argued for a bit and the man threatened to detain Gerald if he didn't leave and let him on with his work. We were scared and didn't know why they were arguing. The man all but pushed Lina's dad out. He shut the door and things got bad pretty quickly. He turned around and knocked Adaleen out, full-on hit her in the face. I went to help her, and he grabbed me and tied up my hands and tied the rope to a hook over a desk. He picked her up and took her to another room. When she woke up, she was..." Jasper looked away from the group, Adaleen stared at the ground drawing in the dirt with a stick...

"She screamed out for me, she kept screaming 'Jasper... Jasper...' I was trying to bite through the ropes. He was hurting her... Then the door busted open, and Gerald came back in looking wild. He tossed a knife at the desk as the other door opened and the man came out. Your dad told me to turn around and I did, and he attacked him. He stabbed and cut and jabbed at him with the knife. The guard was ambushed so quickly he didn't even yell out. He turned me around and I saw how he had cut him. It was methodical almost, he missed anything that would kill him too quickly, but got everything that would leave him helpless, arms gashed deeply at the shoulders, legs and ankles cut to shit, but he was alive, struggling to breathe, just bleeding out. Gerald took me in the room where he had taken Adaleen and she was naked and bleeding, and... he... he locked her up... in a little cage..."

Jasper's voice broke just as Lina gasped suddenly understanding why Jasper hated babies and kids in cages. The realization of why they have been so protective, why Adaleen never went around guys, why jasper hated cages, why they are almost always together as if their clothes were sewn for them to never be part. All of it came at her and she started crying... Feeling foolish she looked at Frills who was running around camp and she tried to hide her tears. How could Lina have never known. How could no one tell her this is why the twins were their family.

"He broke the lock, but I had to coax her out of it... I got her dressed and he took us to his... We popped in and out of there the rest of our lives. Gerald showed us hunting and trapping and self-defense so we could mostly look after ourselves, but they also treated us like family. Yea your pa Gerald Lina, was one of the best men I ever knew." Jasper finished the story and got up to go towards his sister. Adaleen not wanting company rose and walked away from the fire without a word. Dalton sat shocked... He knew there was some story, but he never had considered it would be that dark. Lina removed the now cooked rabbits from the fire as Dalton turned her way.

"Soo, where are your mom and dad then? I know we are heading towards your brother but where did your parents go?" he asked clearly past the embarrassment after his curiosity had been partially sated.

"Well, I guess it was about six years or so ago now," Lina tried to explain thinking back as best she could. "I was running from the kids in town who were making fun of me... they teased me often and had gotten to a point of throwing rocks at me while they did it. I got scared and ran, normally I just ran home but I wanted to go further. Jacob saw me and gave chase yelling out to our father that I had run into the woods. He almost caught me a few times, but I was quicker, so I stayed ahead of him. I didn't think about the fact that the sun was going down until it was dark. Then I was scared so I found a tree stump and tried to hide. Jacob saw me trying to get in it and grabbed me. We turned around and saw three coyotes starting to circle us… Jacob shoved me in the tree stump, and I screamed out. He yelled for our dad and tried to climb in himself while I pulled on him, three more showed up. We were trapped in a dead tree and alone. Then came Dad, he tackled one and Jacob pulled me down, he hid my face so I couldn't see anything happening as he tried to fight them off. But he didn't have enough time to prepare… He didn't have a bow, or the axe… I don't think he even had a knife… He lost. I listened to him yell to Jacob it was all right… I heard him say to take care of us… and then I heard the yells… Jacob put his hands over my ears, but I heard the yells turn to screams… and I heard the screams turn to silence other than them chewing up what was left. The last sound was them dragging his body behind them, and then just me and Jacob crying." Lina looked up at Dalton as he tried to fix his clearly pained face.

"I am so sorry… I feel like all of you have been through so much." He looked from Jasper to Lina as Jasper approached the cooling food.

"Most of your kingdom has stories like ours, Dalton very few live the stories you have," Jasper told him wisely grabbing a rabbit. "Sorry, but I am going to literally track down my sister, I'll be back." Jasper walked off with a rabbit to probably try to get Adaleen to eat.

"What about your mom then? She go stay with a sister or something?" Dalton asked hoping for a lighter story maybe.

"No she disappeared overnight in the same room I was sleeping in. We couldn't find a trace of her or anyone else about or anything missing, just poof, gone," Lina said grabbing the remainder of the rabbit and cutting it in half. She handed half to Dalton and smiled at him. "I know it sounds all bad, but we have had each other to get through all of this which has made it a lot better. I don't know where I'd be without Jasper and Adaleen watching out for me. You shoulda seen what they did to the kids that threw rocks at me that day. One lost an eye... His real eye... We are a family all of us," Lina finished trying to lighten the mood from the pasts depressive hold.

"My mom died when I was really young," Dalton said suddenly. "Queen Love they called her. She was the most beautiful and fairest woman ever. She fell ill randomly and died shortly after. Father was sick with grief for over a year until his new wife showed up. She started making him happy again but she isn't my favorite person. Women that whisper that much to those kinds of people..." Dalton threw up his hands as if it was obvious. "Anyway she had my brother and sister and I'm grateful for that."

He for the first time since they started talking smiled. He started humming a song while he ate his rabbit and looked across at Lina with much regard. Lina didn't know about the Queen Love because she was young then but she was glad that Dalton had someone he could be close to like his brother and sister.

Jasper and Adaleen walked up a bit later looking a bit bedraggled. Adaleen without saying a word sat next to

Lina and laid her head in Lina's lap. Lina softly stroked her hair. Jasper climbed into a nearby tree and looked down at them all.

"We have to get an early start if we don't wanna walk through the night tomorrow so let's call it for the night. I'll take first watch, Dalton are you ready to start after what I showed you today?"

"Yea, vantage points and blind spots and perimeter checks, I got it." He nodded at Jasper.

"All right, Adaleen do you want to sit tonight out and catch up on sleep?" Jasper looked down at his sister who said nothing while Lina stroked her hair.

"Take that as a yes then, Lina you and Adaleen get comfy me and Dalton will be keeping an eye on things," Jasper said as he jumped down from the tree and started looking around. He spotted the bow and arrows and picked them up. Frills moved over to Adaleen, sniffed her then curled up near her chest. Lina took off her jacket and rolled it up for Adaleen to rest her head on and lay behind her. Dalton removed his own jacket and covered them as best he could as Lina held a quietly sobbing Adaleen. Lina held Her until she fell asleep from the warmth, and familiar smell of her closest friend.

Chapter 11

The next morning Lina woke up and found the only noise to be the crackling of the slightly dying fire and soft sounds of Frills snoring. Adaleen had gotten up at some point, and when Lina rose it was to find Jasper, her and Frills alone sleeping at the fire. She started to stretch and look around, when she found Adaleen wrapping a badly burned goose up to be taken with them.

"Jasper will be fine we tried not to burn it, maybe we should be paying more attention to how Lina works the spit in the Fire," Dalton said sitting by the bags of supplies and lacing his boot.

"There is really nothing to it, you just have to watch it and turn it," Lina replied stifling a yawn. "We start moving again today yea?" she asked Adaleen as she stood up and started stretching and adjusting her shirt and pants.

"Yea, we filled the gourds, packed the food and supplies and got the map where we can get to it. We should be ready to go as soon as Jasper wakes," Adaleen told Lina without looking at her.

"Will you walk with me in the woods a moment I need to go..." Lina said suddenly feeling a push on her bladder.

"Sure." Adaleen abandoned the half tied up goose and walked to meet Lina at the tree line. They entered the forest and moved in by the clearing and found a spot for Lina to relieve herself. Adaleen stood by with her eyes sweeping the perimeter.

"I want to start teaching you more self-defense... I think you better be able to use that knife in the future, just in case..." Adaleen mentioned not looking at Lina. Lina remembered the story the night before and agreed without pause. She would do anything to set Adaleen's mind at ease. Lina stood after finishing and fixed her pants. She then walked over to the berry bush and grabbed a few of the now ripe berries. She threw them in her pocket and realized there was something in it. She felt inside and her hand wrapped around her forgotten necklace. She held it up and looked at it. The jewel in the middle caught the light.

"Should we sell this for supplies?" Lina looked at Adaleen who was watching her nearby.

"No, you should keep it, and the earrings," Adaleen said very firmly. Lina considered them a gift from Adaleen like the rest of her attire, she put the necklace back in her pocket and they walked back towards the camp. Jasper was up now as the sun was rising higher.

"All right are we all ready to pack up?" Jasper asked as he and Dalton divide up bags and gourds.

"Yea let's get out of here, who will have the map?" Adaleen asked looking at her brother.

"Well my guess is Dalton can read it best, and he has a knife now so how about we walk with him in front and you behind him with the bow. Then Lina can follow you and I can keep the back of us clear." he looked at all of them thoughtfully before handing Adaleen a bag and gourd. "I will take your extra bag for a while," he added eyeing the bow.

"All right well then let's head off." Dalton had the map in front of him as he started walking carrying his bags and water. Lina ran and scooped up the still sleeping Frills and fell in line behind Adaleen. The bags they had given her were pretty light, so she wasn't worried about the walk as much. Jasper followed her whistling a tune that Lina didn't know.

"We should be able to make it almost past the whole town by the end of the day, we will cut to the left a short way up and continue on to this marker on the map then go right past the town in the woods," Dalton called out from the front.

"Who are you narrating for?" Jasper called up from the back. Dalton looked back and smiled,

"Myself I guess." He laughed as they walked.

After midday they could hear the town on the far right. They had luckily not seen any people even though the prince now wore a cloak he could slide the hood up on, They had other reasons to not want to be seen. Lina noted that the small break they took had healed her feet and she was walking fine again. Actually she felt like her feet never hurt in the beginning at all. They stopped for a moment and split up pieces of the burnt goose to share and fill their audibly hungry bellies. Even Jasper didn't say anything about the bird, though Lina got the distinct feeling he was watching his words around his sister for now. Frills had woken up and been somewhat moody since they left the river. Lina splashed water from her canister on him once, but jasper said to be mindful. If we ran out, someone would be sent to town.

"We are making decent time if we are where I think we are." Dalton studied the map and pointed at a spot. "If we walk into the night, we could make it back to the river."

"No, without a fire we can't be guaranteed a safe night sleeping. Light scares night predators away," Jasper said to him. "We can set up camp just before dark and make it back to the river tomorrow morning. Adaleen you should keep an eye out for any food, Anything at all so we can avoid going into town." Jasper looked meaningfully at his sister.

"You're the one we have to watch in town, what with your drinking and cards and woman..." Adaleen said looking around. "I haven't even seen a bird fly over us, we might just have to grab some more food for the next couple days," she said sighing with defeat. "There just hasn't been any game around here..."

The group walked on in silence for a moment, Frills trotting beside Lina. They could hear the distant town bustling still. People being loud and businesses rolling.

"All right stop," Jasper suddenly said. "Dalton, would you say we are at about a halfway point to where the river is from where we were at?" He looked at Dalton as he looked to the map.

"Yea just about if not a little past," Dalton said looking again at the map.

"Well, I say we go ahead and go buy the extra stuff now, has anyone come up with anything else useful?"

"I mean, a small tent could be a good idea…" Dalton suddenly spoke up then shrugged, "I had been thinking about it."

"We need more arrows, you lost two when you guys went out that only leaves six," Adaleen answered.

"A large metal spit, so we could stop using sticks. Or a pot so I can make soup or broth," Lina added, the group suddenly realizing they could have it a little easier if all chimed in.

"Bigger bags, so we could carry one and not two to three, all right we all have at least one good idea. We have the rest of the day, and we are close to the town. We have over half the money we made, so how about we go a bit deeper in the forest and set up a camp. Then we get some of these last supplies and more food and leave in the morning to make it back to the river and past it?" Jasper proposed.

"Why do you suddenly want to stop again?" Adaleen asked looking at him curiously, "You're changing the whole plan for what?"

"To spare our tired souls of extra work sister, and to maybe try to win us a little more money and get enough stuff that the next week to Mareep isn't hell," Jasper said as innocently as he could muster.

Adaleen looked slightly unconvinced, but nodded all the same. The group walked deeper into the forest till they came to a cluster of large rocks.

"Perfect," Jasper said as he walked into a mini cave and set down his bags. He rifled through them as Adaleen set down hers.

"All right, we will have you two stay here again, and we will nip into town and be back soon," Jasper said suddenly looking like he was in a hurry. Jasper started running about picking up tinder and pieces of dry wood. Dalton began helping as Adaleen started a fire near the opening at the rocks. Adaleen kept looking at her brother curiously. Once the fire was going and a decent pile of tinder and wood had been set to the side, Adaleen and Jasper grabbed their gourds and two bags each and took off towards the town.

"I won't leave you alone this time, but if you're up to it, Adaleen mentioned you may need to learn how to wield your knife a bit better." Dalton looked at Lina as Adaleen and Jasper started to disappear from sight.

"Yes, she thinks it's a good idea... and now that I know more about things, I do too..." Lina added pulling her knife from her sheath.

"Well my swordsman teacher always taught me short blade and knife handling. He said a true swordsman can use any blade; I'm happy to help. Or at least to try to..." Dalton said to her, his eyes meeting her gaze.

"All right..." Lina patted Frills who had curled up by the fire and stood to walk to the space between the trees in front of it. Dalton met her and asked her to take out her knife. Lina did as she was told and held the knife loosely at her side.

"Well, that isn't going to get you anywhere, hold it up like this." Dalton moved her hand up, so her arm was extended out slightly in front of her at an angle. "Your feet need to be about shoulder-length apart so you can hold your ground if you get pushed. It also makes moving around easier so you can push forward or retreat back. "Dalton slid one of Lina's feet to the side.

"Let's practice you holding your stance, now I'm going to try to push you off your stance, okay?"

"Okay, I'm ready," Lina replied putting all her weight in her center and trying to hold it with the knife up. The prince advanced on her and pushed at her shoulder; Lina practically fell completely over.

"Oopse, sorry," Lina said standing up straight again.

"No it's okay, What happened was you were holding your weight at your center not pushing it to your feet. After you get used to the stance, you may be able to hold your center but for now only worry about your footing. What your gunna want to do if you get pushed with too much force, is shuffle back to take some of the force away from the blow, here I'll take the stance and you come at me so I can show you..." Dalton took the stance he had just put Lina in without a knife and she stood in front of him. She waited a moment to try and catch him off guard, and then lurched forward to push his shoulder, the prince shuffled a step back making Lina miss her mark. She attempted to correct and still get him to which he pivoted and pushed her down. Dalton stooped quickly to help her up.

"Are you okay I'm sorry I got carried away." He started wiping dirt off Lina's back.

"No I need to learn how to do that, try me again." She sheathed her knife and took up the position. Dalton reached out to shove her and she shuffled back, he connected, and she was pushed slightly off balance but held her ground.

"That's great, you see when you shuffle back slightly it gives you a slight advantage. My dad always says it's just as important to know when to retreat as when to attack." Dalton looked at her with a smile. "Let's try again."

Lina and Dalton spent the next couple of hours going over different self-defense stances and reactions. He was surprised regularly how she didn't give up and learned quickly. The two sat by the fire after a while and pulled out some stale bread to munch on. Lina lay back rubbing near her bottom where she had landed frequently. She yawned and stretched her arms over her head.

"If you fall asleep this time I won't be leaving so if you wake up and I'm making on a tree, no worries," Dalton said throwing a piece of bread to Frills who sniffed it curiously before swallowing it whole.

Lina lay down a moment and considered taking just a short nap and decided she wasn't that tired and wanted to be sure she slept through the night. She stretched out with her arms under her head and started thinking about the kingdom. She imagined the tall stone pillars and wondered what the king and queen looked like, when all of a sudden, her surroundings got dark.

Lina felt her body almost floating through space as she landed in a large, open clearing. There were flowers everywhere and she seemed to just be on tall grass. She looked to her left and there was the prince she used to dream about, the handsome dark-haired man she had been imagining since she was little. He was wrapped up in writing something and hadn't noticed Lina.

"Am I really here?" Lina asked forcing the man to jump in fright and spill his ink bottle in the grass.

"You again, I thought I'd seen the last of you… but then there was that shadow…" He looked at her curiously. "Are you really here… good question." The man stuck his finger in the ink and reached out to Lina to press it to her cheek just under her eye.

"I can touch you…" he said with surprise. "I wasn't expecting that…" He pulled his hand back slowly, considering what was happening.

"Are you my prince? Where are we?" she asked suddenly looking round and seeing the most beautiful sights she had ever witnessed.

Trees in the far-off distance of soft purple and oranges and yellows, horses running through the grass, and flowers, more flowers than Lina had ever seen before of all colors.

"This is Kingdom Torridity..." The man gestured around him at the woods and flowers, then to the castle that had originally caught Lina's eye. It was made of what Lina could only describe as gems and marble, with huge colorful windows that had pictures of dragons and birds on fire all over them.

"And I am Prince Alucard Of the dragon fae line," said the man looking back to Lina. "And you are the woman I have been dreaming about... are you... the phoenix fae?" Prince Alucard ended his statement looking at Lina curiously.

"I'm just Lina..." Lina responded feeling like he wanted some sort of explanation. "Lina of Crestfallen village..." She finished looking down at her clothes. She seemed to be wearing a soft purple dress made of a slick soft material that felt nice on her skin. "This is not what I was wearing..."

"So you are someplace else then?" Alucard wondered aloud. "I thought for a while I was going mad, then you disappeared..."

"I'm sorry, I don't know how I got here, I'm looking for my brother..." Just as she finished the sentence Lina felt a jerk like being quickly lifted. A bunch of lights seemed to be speeding past her as she flew out of the forest through the air. Lina suddenly felt her body being shaken.

"Lina, Lina are you okay..." Lina raised up and twisted away from Dalton to vomit. He started rubbing her back and handed her his gourd. "What was that... you started almost floating, and your eyes were open, but they looked... different." Dalton looked pale, and she saw Frills sitting near her staring with his head cocked to the side.

"What do you mean different?" Lina asked rinsing her mouth with water and spitting it out.

"Well, you were completely off the ground, and there was this weird purple glow coming off you. Then I saw something in your pocket lighting up. I looked at your eyes and they were open, but they were, well, purple... and they looked like they were shaking... I thought it was some kind of fit... where did this come from?" Dalton reached up and smudged the still slightly wet ink print under Lina's eye. She saw the ink spread on his finger and started questioning everything. She knew her daydreams seemed real, she knew she had been seeing the same man in them for years, since she could remember really...

"Are you going to tell Adaleen and Jasper?" she suddenly asked realizing she had promised to tell Jasper if anything like this came up.

"Lina you were hot to the touch, I started waking you because it looked like you were about to burst on fire. I think they should know in case something is wrong, what if someone put a curse on you or something." Dalton looked at her clearly concerned.

"All right we can tell them tonight when they get back. But please let me explain," said Lina not entirely sure how she was going to explain any of this.

Jasper mentioned her mother having dreams like hers but she never to her recollection floated or heated up. She reached into her pocket remembering that he mentioned something glowing and her hand closed around the necklace. She settled back down by the fire and started wondering what was going on with her.

"A little help please?" Adaleen seemed to be yelling out from the forest. Dalton stood and looked back at Lina for a moment, unsure if he should leave.

"Go ahead," said Lina standing and taking out her knife to practice her stance while he was gone. Dalton left and Lina practiced jabbing at a few trees and watched her footwork, making sure to plant each foot with purpose. She heard a sliding sound and saw Dalton and Adaleen walking up carrying and dragging supplies. She went up to help lighten the load and Adaleen gratefully handed her a few bags.

"Turns out Jasper had a plan the whole time... He took the money and flipped it tripling it in about two card games. Then sent me off to buy some stuff with the winnings while he played. Went back and forth about four times and had more than enough but he said he had to stay, something about it being a lucky day..." Adaleen started to unload and empty the bags near the fire. The first thing she pulled out was some decent leather bags that were big enough to carry twice the amount of stuff as their cloth ones. Next, she pulled a tent out of another bag, and a pot and metal spit for their fires. She went to the last bag and showed them a decent store of dried and salted meats and veggies along with some separately wrapped raw squirrels. Lina noticed the quiver on her back had twice the amount of arrows in it.

The last two bags she reached in and pulled out some new clothes, slacks, and shirts they could change into. She passed out the clothes and started looking for sticks to hold up the metal spit she had bought. After finding them, she dug them into the ground as Lina speared the four squirrels on the spit for roasting. She looked up at Dalton who was watching her closely, waiting for her to bring up the nap.

"When will Jasper be back, I'd like to talk to you both about something," Lina said looking at Adaleen.

"Soon I hope, but who knows... why?" asked Adaleen looking curiously from Dalton to Lina.

"Oh just something he told me to talk to him about if it came up, anyways, Dalton started showing me self-defense moves, come look." Lina rose and moved to the spare spot in the trees and motioned for Adaleen to come over to her, she kept her knife sheathed and planted her feet.

"Try to knock me over..." Lina told her excited to show Adaleen what she learned. Adaleen reached out and just barley attempted to push Lina, she didn't move and barely felt the push.

"No really Adaleen you have to try like it's more serious..." Lina told her standing up and looking at her fiercely. "You have to come at me here..." Lina got back into her stance moving her weight from one foot to the next as Adaleen sighed and lunged out to push Lina. Lina quickly shuffled backwards and dipped to the side of Adaleen's hands, she then put her hand on Adaleen's back and swept a foot under her forcing her to fall on her belly.

"Oh shoot, are you okay?" Lina attempted to rouse Adaleen who was getting to her knees, she looked up at Lina with a huge smile on her face.

"That was great, you were quick and sure about your moves, you must have practiced most of the time we were gone..." Adaleen said rubbing dirt off her knees and slowly rising. "Jasper would be proud of both of you." She regarded Dalton who smiled in the background.

"No trouble even, she is a fast learner... Had me falling over my own moves in no time," Dalton added laughing and rubbing his own bottom where he too had landed quite a few times.

Lina went to the spit and twisted the squirrel so it wouldn't burn. She also went to the bag with food and grabbed a roasted potato. Adaleen went and sat by the fire where Frills and Dalton were already sitting as Lina started describing the different steps and moves, she had been taught.

"You will have to keep practicing till all the moves are natural. You want your body to know what comes before you have to think about it really..." said Dalton to Lina. He looked into the fire then looked back at her curiously.

"Well we will keep her at it until she had gotten better, the sun is getting pretty low—we should start thinking about a sleeping shift. Lina still shouldn't be watching guard just yet." Adaleen looked at the darkening sky and the cooking food.

"After we eat, we should start sleeping in shifts Dalton, I'm hoping Jasper will be back soon but until he arrives it's only us two…" Adaleen looked in the direction of the town and yawned.

"I'll take a nap if you're good then you can wake me up and I'll take a real watch, while you rest up." Adaleen looked to Dalton for approval, he nodded and she looked at the food Lina was turning. Squirrel doesn't take as long as goose and venison because there is so little meat to it. She cooked it up and took it off the spit to cool. She found a rock with a depression in it near the rock formation and filled it with some water from her gourd for Frills, then set some of the squirrel meat beside it. He trotted over and licked her boot before drinking the water and munching on the food.

Lina joined the others around the fire and took her other half a squirrel and her gourd to sit next to Adaleen who was slowly pulling meat away from the squirrel bones with her teeth. The three ate in silence as Frills lapped up the water. After Lina had eaten most of her meat, she lay down. After half a day of walking and a good few hours' real training for the first time ever, plus her random dream travel, she was exhausted. She closed her eyes knowing she would be safe as Frills went to curl up at her chest as usual, she snuggled up to him and the fire and lay in wait to fall into her magical dreams.

Lina woke to arguing that she was pretty used to hearing.

"What are we going to do with a horse, that makes about as much sense as having a cart, it can't handle the hills and cliffs and ups and downs..." Adaleen was saying loudly. Lina opened her eyes to see that Jasper had finally returned.

"Let's see, we can lighten out load for carrying have a speedy getaway for two people, be able to scout ahead when we aren't sure where we want to go... honestly sis you act like this was a bad idea."

"How did you get enough gold for a horse? There is no way you won that much at cards." Adaleen put her hand to her head like she was in physical pain trying to make sense of her brother.

"I won the horse in a card game fair and square, I don't know why but I had a feeling I had to play cards like I was going to end up getting something I need..." Lina stopped listening to Jasper talking to Adaleen and looked at the horse as Frills uncurled and yawned next to her.

"I also got three raw pheasants so we can actually eat before we leave," Jasper ended his explanation. "Oh and I almost forgot..." He pulled a sword out of a holster that the horse was carrying.

"For you Dalton, not the best, but it's all we could get for now." Jasper handed the blade to Dalton, who whipped it around him expertly in a flash. Jasper went to the fire and built it up a bit with a bag still slung over his shoulder. He started pulling the pheasants out of the bag and lining them up on the spit then threw it up over the fire. Lina looked over at Dalton, who suddenly looked away from her.

"Jasper…" Lina said timidly… "I have to talk to you and Adaleen about those daydreams," she finished quickly trying to make it sound unimportant. Jasper looked at Dalton, then slowly dragged his eyes to Adaleen. She locked eyes with him and abandoned the horse she had been looking over to join the others at the fire.

"Now then what is there to talk about?" Jasper asked looking directly in Lina's eyes.

"I wasn't completely honest with you… my dreams have been really vivid lately… and yesterday for the first time in a while I had a daydream. Except I'm not sure that's what it really is… I was talking to a person and wearing different clothes, but he reached out and put this dot of ink under my eye… Then a moment or so later I woke up and well, maybe you should let Dalton tell you what he saw while I was… gone," she finished in a hurry not really knowing how to explain this to them.

"Gone…" Jasper asked looking curiously at Dalton… "She left?"

"No… she was there but she was different. One second, she was stretched out staring off at the tree tops the next she was… well floating… and her hair was wild and there was this glow coming off of her. I went and looked at her and her eyes were open, and they had turned purple, and she had heat coming off of her. Her eyes were shaking back and forth, and she was getting hotter, that's when I saw the ink mark appear under her eye. I got scared and started trying to wake her up..." Dalton finished looking at the twins for any sign they knew this would happen.

"This is not good..." Jasper looked at his sister and told her.

"We knew she was different like her mom, Jacob told us forever ago, we just need to keep a closer eye... and you Lina," Adaleen suddenly addressed Lina. "You have to control your daydreams, you can't let just anyone see that or they will try to burn you for witchcraft."

"I'm usually too tired to daydream any more, I just have the really vivid dreams of another place. I wonder if they are all Kingdom Torridity..." she mused aloud.

"Kingdom Torridity?" Dalton asked suddenly fear-struck.

"Yes, that is where Prince Alucard is. According to my last dream,'" Lina answered looking at him.

"Do you know where it is?" She suddenly felt a rush of excitement, she hadn't thought to ask this before.

"Yes... It's to the east of our kingdom past the dense magical forest. People don't travel there any more, The kingdom of the fae is very dangerous for us."

Lina considered his words as she checked the pheasants. They were quite finished, so she pulled them from the fire and propped the spit up for them to cool.

"Are you lot packed and ready to go after breakfast?" Jasper asked looking at the group quickly.

"We will eat load up the horse and ourselves and take off, we will make good ground not having to carry everything ourselves... and I'll feel better talking about this dream issue once we are farther away from people, honestly..." Jasper told the group as they all sat pondering the kingdom far away and what Lina had to do with it.

The group packed up their belongings as they waited for their food to cool. Lina went and put more water in the rock for Frills who had been watching everyone since he had woken up looking groggy still. She gave him some pheasant and potatoes and he eagerly gobbled it up, while she replaced her boots.

They sat around the fire eating quickly with all their stuff ready to go when they heard a twig snap and footsteps approaching...

"Right everybody ready? Let's take off..." Jasper suddenly stood and made to grab the horse while everyone looked at him in surprise. Just then about three men started running towards the group in the distance.

"Jasper what have you done now..." Adaleen said as she kicked dirt on the fire and ran to scoop up Frills who was running around in circles trying to catch his tail. Lina and Dalton were quick to their feet and started following after Jasper who was pulling the horse at a quick trot.

"I didn't do anything swear on Ma and Pa, some people are just sore losers sis," Jasper hollered back to Adaleen who was bringing up the back of the group.

"Ayy cheater, come back here with my horse..." The men were running but falling behind fast as Lina and the group ran from the spot into the forest.

"Jasper did you really cheat?" Dalton laughed jumping on a raised tree root and lunging forward off it, as Lina leaped over the root followed closely by Adaleen.

"I told you, no *'they just play cards like a horse's arse'*," Jasper yelled the last part and laughed as the group followed him across the forest losing the men in the run. They ran until the sounds of being followed faded and slowed to catch their breath as they continued their journey towards the schooling town of Mareep.